"What are you thinking?"

Would it be the mature thing to tell him the truth?

But what did she
telling him the t

A voice within h
Max Rickman's
loved him but bec   he hadn't loved her
when Elena was conceived. And that was a
completely childish desire.

"I was thinking abou…what happened
between us. After the fire," she admitted. "I
keep blaming you, and it's not fair because
I knew your girlfriend had just died. I took
advantage of you as much as you did of me."

Max raised his eyebrows. "That's a new and
interesting take on it."

"Isn't it," she agreed.

"I'd been attracted to you," he said, "before
Salma died. To be honest, I'm attracted now."

Dear Reader,

Of all traditional romance plots, I've always been most mystified by "secret baby" stories. I've been told by counsellors that it does happen – for one reason or another, a pregnant woman decides not to tell the father of her child about their baby. Part of writing stories is learning what motivates people. I enjoyed writing *Because of Our Child* and getting to understand both the mother and father of this child, Elena, but especially Elena herself.

I've heard friends speak with lingering resentment of being denied time with a father because of bitterness between divorced parents. I've seen the pain of children denied time with a parent for the same reason.

This book is a wish for peace and mutual respect between parents at war and for children who find themselves in the midst of such conflict. It is an acknowledgement of the crucial place of his or her father in the life of every child.

Wishing you all good things always…

Sincerely,

Margot Early

Because of
Our Child

MARGOT EARLY

MILLS & BOON

Pure reading pleasure

*First published in Great Britain 2008
by Harlequin Mills & Boon Limited,
Eton House, 18-24 Paradise Road, Richmond, Surrey TW9 1SR*

© Margot Early 2007

ISBN: 978 0 263 86162 4

38-0608

*Harlequin Mills & Boon policy is to use papers that are
natural, renewable and recyclable products and made from
wood grown in sustainable forests. The logging and
manufacturing processes conform to the legal environmental
regulations of the country of origin.*

*Printed and bound in Spain
by Litografía Rosés S.A., Barcelona*

PROLOGUE

July 23
Thirteen years ago
Makal Canyon, California

THEY HAD NO TIME. The screaming roar blasted its heat at their backs, and the ridge where they'd thought they could deploy their fire shelters was too far away. Jen had already dropped her pack and everything but her Pulaski—the unique fire-fighting tool that was a cross between a pickax and an ax—her canteen and her shelter. She'd removed the last from its case and had partially unfolded it. Behind her, abandoned gas cans exploded and tree limbs cracked and blew apart.

It would be quick, Jen knew—she would inhale flames and asphyxiate. She could lie down now, and soon it would be over.

No, not lie down. There would be better air

near the ground. If she lay down, the fire might skip over, burning her, and then the end would be slow and painful.

In any case, it wasn't an option now, because Max was dragging her on. Max Rickman, the squad boss, worked with the Santa Inez Hotshots to pay for graduate school. One of the other hotshots, Salma Garcia, who was also a grad student, had just become Max's fiancée. For Jen and her sister, Teresa, as for Max and his fiancée, fighting fires provided money for school. Jen was an undergraduate at the University of California, Santa Barbara, headed for a Bachelor of Arts in Liberal Studies, combining dance, communications and film studies; and Teresa was saving for medical school, which she planned to begin that fall.

They were close, all the Santa Inez Hotshots, most of them living next door to each other in two households during the off-season and so much like a family that Jen found it amazing to think that Max and Salma had managed a romance.

Though Max Rickman probably could make any woman, other than a dead one, consider marriage.

Max had a fusee, a fire-starting device, in his hand, and Jen watched him light a blaze upwind of them. The grass ignited, seemed to explode, and then he dragged Jen on, into the area he'd burned ahead of them. She felt the soles of her boots separate from the uppers as she heard Max shout, "Deploy!"

She understood what he'd done—creating a safe black zone. Her fear seemed to make all the heat one, all the flames one. As she dropped her Pulaski, the wind tore her shelter from her hands.

Now I'm going to die.

Max had already shaken out his shelter, two paces ahead of her; Jen sensed others following. Shelters appeared around her as branches blew through the air.

Where was Teresa? With the other group, just as Salma was, cutting fire line to the east. They would be safe. They had to be.

The squad boss pushed her into his shelter, against its interior, pressing himself against her and securing the left strap with his left arm. With gloved hands, Jen helped push out the walls, knowing that Max Rickman had just increased his own odds of dying or being burned. She felt Max check that her long braid was inside her clothing, and then he covered the back of her head and the back of his. Faces down, heads together and farthest away from the approaching flames, hard hats banging, they waited, and then there was no time to wait.

We're dying, anyhow.

It was as if she'd stuck her head inside a jet engine. No, her whole body, because the wind ripped at the shelter, trying to yank it away as she tried to hold down her side. She realized that Max didn't trust her completely and was taking care of that for himself.

"Keep away from the edges!"

Did she imagine his voice, that baritone? She tried to make herself small, to give them both more air and hence more insulation. But it all seemed absurd, unreal. It was too hot. She was burning. She heard screaming. Then, someone praying. One of the guys. Loud, low.

I'm supposed to breathe or meditate or think of some religious image...

It was not difficult to believe in God, because it had to be something divine to be so powerful. The fire was the universe's loudest voice, she thought, pointing out that she was nothing and that whether she lived or died, her soul was owned and owing.

And then, when the noise lessened and when the shelter, their dark pod, had stopped shaking and screaming around them, she heard people talking—and one of them was Max. "Everyone, resist the urge to find out if it's any better outside. I guarantee it's not."

Some light had begun to filter through their shelter.

"Where are the other guys?" someone asked. "Did it go up the east side?"

Where Salma and Teresa were.

"I'm definitely burned," another hotshot said.

Jen thought she was, too, on the backs of her calves, but she wasn't certain. The fire had shot small holes through the shelter, and it felt as though pinpoint embers were singeing her, stinging her with sharp points of intense heat. She didn't make a sound, because she was a person who dealt with pain internally. Her burns, she thought, could not be bad.

"You burned, Max?" she said.

"Oh, maybe a bit."

"Where's Jen? Her shelter blew away."

That was Frey, one of their sawyers.

"She's right here with me," Max said.

"Max, you dog."

And someone said, "The gulch was too steep. Everything was too steep."

LuAnn, a Texas native, said, "I'm gonna pray, you guys." She began the Lord's Prayer and she knew all the words, and Jen said them in her head, too, thinking that Teresa might be dead and Salma might be dead and Salma's fiancée had just risked his life to save her, Jen Delazzeri.

But the others had been in a better spot, closer to a safety zone, closer to good black.

"It's always handy," Max said, after the amen, "when someone knows their prayers."

It had to be a hundred and twenty degrees inside the shelter. Jen reached her canteen, took a sip, and shared the remaining water with Max. It had begun to lighten outside, and now she saw his long dark lashes and brown eyes, so dramatic and unusual against his white-blond hair, now covered in soot and ash.

Jen said, "Do you believe in God?"

"Ask me later."

And she knew that he was thinking of his lover. Of Salma.

CHAPTER ONE

Silver Jack Ridge
Colorado
June

JEN DELAZZERI DID NOT WANT to cover fires for Channel 4. Any of the fires. And this year there were many.

Fires were the story of the summer, but so far she'd managed to get away with simply interviewing fire managers from time to time. The smell of the smoke and the haze in the air were the same smoke and haze experienced by everyone else in Colorado in that summer of fire and drought—everyone else, that is, who wasn't close to a blaze. The fire situation in the Front Range, around Denver, had been less extreme than that in the western part of the state. It had seemed likely that Jen could live out the summer reporting water rationing and the effect of smoky air on historical monuments and on people with compromised respiratory systems.

But suddenly her reprieve was over.

On Silver Jack Ridge, two smoke jumpers had been entrapped and had died. Today, the following day, the fire continued to burn out of control, covering almost two thousand acres. Now, outfitted in green fire-retardant pants and a yellow fire shirt like the firefighters, Jen sat aboard a helicopter. For the camera, she let her long hair, thick, dark and curly, spill down her back, though she'd already told the camera crew she was getting that hair inside her clothing at the first sign of a spark. Like the firefighters, she also wore a hard hat, and on her feet were leather boots for the helicopter ride toward Silver Jack Lake and Silver Jack Ridge, in an area called the Sawtooth Range.

For Channel 4—and for a chance at a spot on network television—Jen had agreed to do this, to land in the thick of the danger. Her first jobs in television had been with small local stations. She'd had to lug camera equipment, *everything,* herself. In Colorado, that had often meant driving to obscure lo-

cations to interview, well, eccentric char-
acters.

And she was making decent money, now.
Not great, but enough.

But not enough for this. She didn't want
to ask any of the questions that needed to be
asked. Because if she asked the questions,
she'd become angry. Angry at fire supervisors who had let the situation develop. Angry
at herself for asking firefighters questions
they shouldn't have to answer, for voicing
criticism they should never have to hear.

For instance, she would have to mention
Storm King Mountain, the South Canyon
fire of 1994, in which fourteen firefighters
had died. She would have to ask fire personnel if there were similarities between the
situations; and she already knew the answer
to that, had seen aerial photographs. The
steep terrain, the gulleys. Mann Gulch,
Storm King…Makal Canyon, though the
loss of life there had been smaller. That had
been eclipsed by the greater tragedy in
Colorado that same summer.

Jen wanted no part of any of it.

In the helicopter, she peered through the
glass and jotted notes on a pad. Over the

years, she'd found the practice to be calming, an anchor for her in highly charged situations. Focusing on paper, forming questions, anticipating all the paths the answers might take, kept her anxiety at bay. Later she would take refuge in her own presence in front of the camera, her voice, her posture.

Notes to herself from life outside work crowded the borders of the pad, perpendicular to her fire notes.

Call River Spirit Dance Supply. An 800 number. That was for Elena's new dance clothes, promised for the new school year still months away. After the inevitable dispute about how much it was reasonable to spend, and whether two crop tops were truly enough for a sixth-grader who danced every single day.

Elena's dancing every single day was no problem for Jen. Aside from being convenient—her daughter was occupied while she herself was at the station and on assignments—Elena had chosen an interest, no, an obsession, that Jen could understand. It was only in the years after Makal Canyon that Jen herself had moved away from dance. Her subsequent interest in martial arts had come around the time her daughter was two—a reaction to many things, not least the fire the she had survived before Elena was conceived.

Jen had finished school not at UCSB, where she'd begun, but at UCLA, with much of her course work completed at USC. Teresa had been in medical school at UCLA, at first, so it had made sense. Jen had switched to film, then back to dance and then into journalism, floundering while giving the appearance of succeeding, maintaining a 4.0 average because she had been spared, because her life mattered and had to matter. And nothing she did would ever be enough to compensate for the fact that she had made it, that she had survived the Makal Canyon fire. That even her sanity had survived.

Because of her experience in that long-ago California fire, she knew that there might be more value in interviewing members of the fire crew than managers, especially because now that mistakes had been made, the top brass, those known collectively as "overhead," were no doubt rushing to cover up anything that had been done wrong.

She was to meet with the incident commander, who'd been relieved, and his replacement. She checked her notes, to get their names right, and scanned the names of the dead and those of the jump crew who remained on the mountain, fighting without their fallen comrades.

It was then she saw his name.

Max Rickman.

A survivor again.

MAX SUCKED ON HIS CANTEEN for a brief moment before applying his Pulaski to the brush that needed to be cleared in order to create a new helicopter landing site. The original helispot was still safe, but it was too far from the jump crew and hotshots remaining on Silver Jack Ridge—as was the place he'd suggested for the second helispot. So they were here instead.

Two Montana smoke jumpers and one from New Mexico worked with him to clear the brush. The four of them were all that remained of the first load of six who had jumped to the Silver Jack fire seventy-two hours before.

From the moment he arrived, Max had found this terrain reminiscent of other death traps he'd known or known of. What had seemed different—and reassuring—was the fire, which was small and of a reasonable size for two teams of smoke jumpers. On the ground, however, the similarities to previous disasters became more obvious. An under-qualified incident commander, and no good way to get the job done. Crews placed in what were, in hindsight, bad positions to fight the fire.

Then, everything had gone wrong.

Shifting winds.

Safe spots that turned unsafe.

Now, two jumpers were dead, their remains still lying where they'd fallen, pending the investigation of the fire.

Max was alive because he had said no.

He'd been uneasy working that far out on the ridge, in such difficult terrain with so much grass on top of it, regardless of the apparent quiet of the fire in the box canyon below. He had agreed, instead, to work with a forest service crew circling the fire below.

The Montana jumpers, including his own jump partner Alex Tock, and John Jackson from New Mexico, had repeated Max's protest and fallen into work with him.

This was Max's eighteenth season fighting fires. The Santa Inez Hotshots—seasonal firefighters, as were the smoke jumpers, with other lives and other jobs the rest of the year—had split up after the Makal Canyon blaze. As had been known to occur among other crews after similar tragedies. More than one of their number had quit the work.

But Max had realized, for the first time, that he never wanted to quit.

He stopped thinking, except to check the horizons for smoke and watch the progress of the fire. He swung the Pulaski in rhythm, against the sound of a chain saw operated by a forest service firefighter who'd joined them at the new helispot.

The rotors of the arriving chopper made a thud-thud-thud that he actually felt before he first heard the higher chattering of the helicopter's rotors. He'd tried to discern, over the years, whether he actually sensed the helicopters through his feet, if they made a vibration in the ground that could be felt before they were sensed in any other way.

He always knew when one was coming before others heard it, and a Vietnam veteran who had become a fire supervisor had told Max he wasn't unusual in that ability.

He and the other jumpers and firefighters at the helispot cleared their tools from the new landing zone and watched as the chopper set down and a flight crew member, then a passenger, climbed out.

"That," said Tock, beside Max, "must be the media."

The visitors were another sore spot, as far as Max was concerned, and the other firefighters agreed with him. Nothing was predictable about this fire, and it was one place a television news crew, even a crew of two—reporter and cameraman—didn't belong.

The woman who'd come out first was going to have to get that long hair tucked away to start with. Who had allowed this? But he answered Tock, deadpan. "Maybe she's a rookie."

The individual in question, who now had the attention of every man there, had a straight, elegant nose, a curling cascade of thick, dark hair, well-defined black brows and a smile that was radiant in its suddenness as she turned to speak to one of the helicopter crew.

Max knew the smile.

Their eyes met across the helispot.

No way. As a crew member gestured the

path she should take away from the chopper, Max stepped toward her. "Jen?"

She turned, her woman's face more austere, remote and wary than the nineteen-year-old face had ever been. But her smile seemed genuine. "Max!" She hugged him.

Keeping an arm around her waist, he guided her further away from the chopper, through the smoky haze of the helispot. "Did you come to relieve us?"

"No. I came to ask questions. Channel 4. Denver."

His objections to civilians at the site vanished. "I've smudged you."

Jen glanced down at her fire shirt and shrugged. She was her own makeup woman out here, and she would deal with her face and the rest of her appearance before she went on camera. She was calm; Max shouldn't be able to tell that her muscles were strung tight. She wanted him to know that it was no problem for her, seeing him after all these years. None at all. "You look the same," she said.

"Covered in soot."

"Yes." With the whites of his eyes still showing extraordinarily bright, even when bloodshot from smoke. The irises were the shade of dark chocolate—or darker, almost black. And the blond hair—now more straw-colored, more golden than pale blond—was comparatively short. But really, he looked the same.

She remembered something, remembered that if they stood facing each other, her lips could just touch the base of his throat.

That would not have changed, either.

Of course, she wasn't planning on testing the memory to see if it was accurate.

"What questions are you going to ask?"

Jen considered whether or not to answer him. But what had Max done to deserve being surprised by her inquiry? "I'll want to know what happened yesterday. I'll have to ask if there are any similarities between yesterday's events and what happened at Storm King Mountain in 1994."

"Why don't you talk to the IC?" The incident commander.

"Well, I will. But I'll also want to speak with the firefighters. We're covering the fire for the news, but we may include some footage as part of an hour-long special we're planning on wildfire."

"Going to give Nova a run for its money?"

As part of her preparation, Jen had watched

Nova's *Fire Wars*. "No. We're taking a different angle. World fire, actually."

"And you're covering western Colorado?"

"Yes." She barely noticed the quiet ribbing about this small corner of the world. No need to explain how surprisingly uncomplicated she'd found the assignment, in the end. No need to say that Elena was attending a dance camp in nearby Ouray this week.

No need to mention Elena, at all.

As a matter of fact, it was easy not to think of Elena. Because this smoke, at close range, was part of her intimate memory, much more so than the smoke she'd smelled in Denver and elsewhere on the Front Range throughout the summer. She had breathed this smoke before.

"Where are you based?" she asked Max. "Still in California?"

He shook his head. "Leadville."

Her intake of breath was involuntary. He had been that close… For how long?

Smoke jumpers weren't like hotshots. They didn't necessarily stay together all fire season. Many of them spent their winters in Montana, employed by the government sewing packs or other fire equipment. Others worked different jobs altogether. "What do you do in the off-season?" she asked.

The chopper rose into the air, startling her. She hadn't expected to be left on the ridge without transport. Max's radio crackled and he cocked an ear, listening.

She heard it, too; someone requesting a water drop.

Of course, this was too far from Denver to use the station's helicopter, so she and her cameraman had flown in on a chopper belonging to the Bureau of Land Management. Nothing about her experience in Makal Canyon had increased her confidence in that federal agency or made her happy to be in their keeping. She had no doubt whatsoever about the pilot's credentials—he was ex-military and better than competent. It was just the matter of what the BLM might ask him to do.

And apparently, now he was fulfilling a new request, to leave Channel 4 at the helispot and make a water drop.

Oh, well.

By her watch it was just after 3:00 p.m. They should get to work filming. The new incident commander was supposed to meet them here. "Is Hugh Barlow here?" she asked Max, who hadn't yet answered her question about how he spent the off-season.

"Don't know him."

"He's the new IC."

"I haven't yet met him."

Jen's journalistic instincts kicked in. This wasn't the story Channel 4 wanted. Nothing incendiary, the station manager had instructed her, with a wink, that was supposed to drive home his stupid pun. She detested the man, who was given to a form of harassment that didn't quite qualify legally as sexual harassment. Until recently. Outside of work, he had come on to her in a way she'd found so offensive—and disturbing—that she'd wondered about her future with Channel 4. Even his *nothing incendiary,* wink, wink, was now tinged for her with knowledge she truly wished she didn't have of him.

She was supposed to present a supportive look at the nearly impossible job everyone, from overhead in public agencies to the lowliest firefighter, was attempting to perform: to keep every one of these blazes from destroying property and taking lives.

She wasn't supposed to find out what anyone had done wrong on the Silver Jack Ridge fire. And she'd believed, when she'd left Denver, that she'd have no trouble following those instructions. She knew the kinds of things that people could do wrong fighting wildfire, and she'd seen the results, smelled the results, lived some of the results. She was no Norman or John Maclean, dedicated to exposing mistakes. Others—fire investigators, other journalists—could do that.

But Hugh Barlow had taken over as incident commander that morning at eight-thirty. Surely Max would at least know what he looked like by now. "Who's the smoke jumper in charge?"

"I am. Today."

As she'd thought. He'd been a squad boss at Makal Canyon. She estimated that he'd been fighting fires for almost twenty years. He was not incident commander on this fire, nor had he been at any time. Smoke jumper in charge was a position that came with its own responsibilities. So what did *today* mean?

But she had the answer. It was in her notes. The smoke jumper in charge yesterday had died yesterday.

Bob Wright, her cameraman, joined them, and Jen introduced Max.

Bob squinted at the chopper and hoisted his camera to his shoulder, training it on their departing transportation.

Jen turned to her own bag, her own gear, for a quick makeup check before clipping on a microphone.

Okay, so she wouldn't dig up the mistakes that had led to yesterday's deaths. But she wouldn't cover them up, either.

She wasn't yet ready to turn to work. She had questions, yes, but they were for Max Rickman the man, not Max the smoke jumper.

Peering at her reflection and seeing the backdrop haze of smoke, she said, "Why are you still in fire?"

"How could I not be?"

Glancing up, she saw him gaze away, as though into the distant past.

Surely, surely, he did not still pine after his dead fiancée.

"You haven't married?" she asked.

He shook his head. Eyed her. "You?"

"No." A definite response, with the vigor of a lie; a lie that proclaimed she would have nothing to do with marriage or commitment or anything associated with those things. A lie that said she was too free to have children, for instance. Of course, there was nothing to hide, and even if he met Elena Jen doubted he would suspect or think or see.

"How's Teresa?" he asked.

"Mm, good." Vague, intentionally vague. And truthful. *Good* meant *good as compared to very bad,* of which Max was probably unaware.

When Jen glanced up at his face again, she saw that he was watching a column of smoke rising from below. He lifted his radio and reported it. She was sure she hadn't seen it from the air; sure it hadn't been there minutes earlier. The afternoon seemed to her windless, unaccountably warm.

Jen knew from studying maps and reports that the smoke jumpers who had died the day before had died because of a sudden reversal of wind at the edge of the ridge, with a box canyon below. Experienced men dying in an unpredictable—and yet appallingly predictable—situation.

The odds against what she sensed happening now should have comforted her.

She and Bob had been equipped with fire

shelters but they hadn't been instructed in their use. She knew the shelters had changed since she and Max had shared one so many years before. And Bob wouldn't have a clue what to do.

She said, "Bob, if we get into trouble, you'll have to leave the camera."

He gaped at her. They'd found themselves in bad spots before. There had been that sniper in Lodo, for instance. And when they'd had to cover the airplane crash....

But he would not leave the digital video camera. His expression said she could just forget that possibility, because whatever happened he would want to record it.

She followed Max's gaze as the wind came, darkening the smoke column, which seemed to separate and come together again, as flame emerged and sudden gusts cast sparks from the top of a piñon below into what looked like gambel oak, the infamous Storm King killer.

"Escape fire," said Tock, and Max drew out a fusee.

Jen understood. The smoke jumpers on the helispot set fire to the grass, that which hadn't been cleared from the helispot, to create a "safe black zone," an area that had already been burned and thus would be a safe place to escape the fire coming toward them.

Bob filmed the smoke jumpers and Jen checked her microphone, clipped into Bob. "We're at a newly established helispot below Silver Jack Ridge, and flames are erupting below us. Smoke jumpers are setting an escape fire, creating a safety zone where we can retreat. We're wondering if they're going to ask us to shelter up."

Max, across the helispot, heard her and nodded—an answer.

There was no way the camera and Bob and she would all fit in one shelter, and she knew she wasn't going to be able to persuade Bob to put down that damned camera. Also, if they were going to deploy shelters, now was the time. She lifted Bob's shelter from the pack strapped to his waist. It unfolded easily. "Bob, for God's sake, set down the camera, lie down and keep the edges of this shelter down. The open part is on the bottom."

"We're going to shelter up on this hot ash, with our feet to the blaze," Jen said for the benefit of the tape. "Smoke jumpers are directing us to shelter locations."

"I'll take this, fools," said a smoke jumper beside them, tugging the heavy camera and its straps from a protesting Bob and gathering the microphone from Jen. "Get in those shelters now."

This isn't happening.

It was unlikely for a firefighter to be caught in more than one entrapment situation. And Jen was no longer even a firefighter.

Watching Bob take direction on getting into his shelter, she pulled out her own. Max's eyes locked with hers for just a moment, as he walked over beside her and yanked out his.

As she lay down, pulling the shelter over her, she noticed him arranging his shelter next to hers.

The job, she thought. She could keep doing her job with the handheld digital recorder she sometimes used when she was driving.

Inside a shelter, a tin foil house.

The roar erupted, and she remembered a

much younger Max Rickman beside her, their unwashed bodies so close in the searing heat.

She wished—and could not believe she wished it—that he was with her now, inside this shelter.

"Hold down the edges, Jen!"

A baritone shout amid the roaring flames, or a voice from her memory.

"The fire is coming over us," she said with the voice recorder against her mouth. "It's hot in here, really hot, but not as bad as it is outside. These new shelters are an improvement on the old ones. Yes, I'm terrified. Someone is screaming." She made herself continue to report. "I'm not sure who it is. My cameraman is to my left and smoke jumper Max Rickman on my right. The screams sound farther away." *I don't want it to be burns.* "It's uncomfortably hot. I'm trying to hold down this shelter, but the fire, I think, has punched some small holes in it. I'm not going to look up for any reason. I'm drinking some water. That's what's recommended when you're in a burnover." *And how do you know this, Jen Delazzeri?*

"Bob, drink water!" she yelled, but how could anyone hear?

She remembered the sensation from Makal Canyon. The unbearable heat.

But this time it was not quite as intense.

Yet the screaming was coming from somewhere.

Someone was burned.

I don't want to know. I don't want to be here. Who picked this helispot?

A cry erupted from her, into the roar.

Only the darkness and heat answered, the wind ripping at the sides of the shelter, trying to tear it apart and incinerate her.

Then, the lighter world, the quieter place. What had she screamed, and had she been heard?

"Bob, talk to me!" Through the heat.

"I'm here, Jen!"

"My cameraman is talking to me from his shelter. He surrendered the camera to one of the smoke jumpers. I don't know what's happened to it. The fire has taken about five minutes to pass over us, but it's quieter now and lighter inside the shelters. I don't think I've been burned."

"Channel 4, stay in your shelters!" A commanding voice, a baritone. "Tock!"

"I'm here."

"Bob, did you hear that? Stay in the shelter!"

"I'm not going anywhere."

Radios squawked.

"The smoke jumpers," Jen told the recorder, told those who might sometime hear the recording, "are equipped with radios and are talking to each other. Someone's hurt, and they're trying to learn who. We need to stay in the shelters because of the dangerous gasses and lack of oxygen outside after the burnover."

"Jen?"

Max's voice.

"Yes."

"You okay?"

"Yes. Are you?"

"Yes."

Like a long time ago.

The radios making noise.

When they got out of these shelters, they would see who was hurt and how badly, and she would report it, but Bob would film delicately.

Oh. No camera, though. How could it have escaped?

What she wished *she* could escape, now and forever, was a baritone voice from her past and the remembrance of need.

CHAPTER TWO

IT WASN'T OVER. Jen knew better than to risk peeking out from under the edge of her shelter. That was, perhaps, for Max to do.

Yet she was unprepared for the new surge of wind and heat. It took time for her to understand what was happening. As she did, she remembered her tape recorder, still running because the sounds outside had never stopped.

Roaring air.

Screams from that one firefighter.

"What passed over us before was the crown fire. Now the grass is burning." If the tape recorder picked up her voice, it would be a miracle.

She remembered, abruptly, the disgusting sexual advances of Gary Lowell, the station manager. As the heat inside her shelter grew again, she sipped water and thought, *Life is too short to be around that man.* Granted, he would do nothing inappropriate on the job, but she had had too many unpleasant encounters with him. What if she gave notice and took a job elsewhere?

How much longer did she have in this job, anyway? Should she be switching to radio, perhaps?

I can't burn up. Who will take care of Elena?

Her own mother would, of course. *Like she's capable of taking care of anyone, Jen. As though Teresa is, either.* But the judgment wasn't entirely fair; didn't take in the whole picture. They had lived together, three generations of women, since not long after Elena's birth. The arrangement had made it possible for Jen to graduate from college.

She sipped water, and said to the deafening wind buffeting the edge of her shelter, "The heat in here is nearly intolerable. I can feel the grass fire around us. Grass fires burn more quickly, thank God."

Finish burning. Finish burning.

A corner of her shelter whipped up, and flame was inside. She screamed, and then rolled—instinctively trying to smother the fire, while also trying to drag down the back of the shelter. Her pants had burned off a buttock and the back of one thigh, yet the violent shaking of the shelter had ceased, and Jen rolled and squirmed, trying to put out a fire that seemed to be on the roof of the shelter.

"Jen?"

Max's voice. Again. Because it was quiet. No, not quiet; just no longer deafening.

"The fire got inside. I've put it out. I'm okay."

"Burned?" he asked.

Inside his shelter, Max heard Tock's voice on his radio, saying, "Wild Thing?"

"I'm here." Tock called him Wild Thing because of a children's book about a boy named Max, whose mother had called him Wild Thing.

"You watching a clock?"

"I am." Max had spent most of the time in his shelter remembering times precisely. What had happened, and when, would matter to fire investigators.

"Yes," said Jen, finally answering Max's question. *Burned?*

This was why civilians, non-firefighters,

were not welcome around blazes like the Silver Jack Ridge fire.

"Not bad," she added. But it hurt like hell.

From his shelter, Max heard her talking to someone else, and then he realized that she must have a tape recorder with her.

"How's your cameraman?" he asked.

They continued talking, all of them, by radio and by shouts. A smoke jumper from New Mexico was the one who'd been burned. Max felt a strange emotion, one he'd known before—that the fire had missed him again, that he'd been passed over, only to save him for another death that might be worse or might come in old age. When were these things evened out?

Fire had caught Jen Delazzeri. Jen, who'd never fought another fire, he knew, after Makal Canyon.

Something bad in store for me, he thought and then stopped imagining. He concentrated, instead, on his job. Raising the chopper, requesting medical evacuation for at least two.

Then, he lifted the edge of his shelter.

Good air.

Wind lifted the aluminum lifesaver away from him.

He saw Tock emerge from silver, across the haze of the blackened, incinerated helispot, and he rattled the shelter beside his. "Jen?"

He let her lift up the shelter, and then the wind flipped it over.

The back of her thigh and one buttock were burned, second-degree, he guessed from the blistering.

She was not one for making noise. She asked, "How bad is it?"

"Not bad. Drink water and stay put for now." She would have to be treated for shock.

But Jackson, the New Mexico jumper, was in worse shape and in far more danger.

Failure. Max's failure. Not to speak up when the helicopter landed; before it landed.

But he'd seen nothing below them, then.

Jackson was making muffled sounds that Max associated with bravely borne agony.

There were six of them at the helispot and not much water to be spared, to pour over the third-degree burns on Jackson's legs and back.

His radio crackled: "Max, we can't get a chopper to you until those winds calm down."

That wind pushing him, attempting to

move him, Max stepped away from Jackson to tell the IC, whom he now knew by voice, if not by sight, that they had someone with third-degree burns over forty percent of his body and the newscaster had first- and second-degree burns over maybe six percent.

The priority was to preserve life, and Jackson's was in danger.

He had not seen Salma after Makal Canyon blew up. She'd been airlifted to a hospital in Denver, and they were apart when she died the following day.

But Jen's sister, Teresa, had been with Salma the whole time.

Max was the one who should have been there.

He returned to Jackson, through the flapping sounds made by everything that was flying about in the wind.

Tock was ready to walk to find water, and Max nodded at him to go. The creek was not far down the slope, and Jackson needed more water. Max emptied his own canteen over Jackson's burns, ignoring what he was seeing—not the burns, but Jackson's body position, curled over a large black object.

Jackson, you chivalrous idiot, he thought.

"It got under the shelter," Jackson said when Max crouched beside him. He meant the flames, Max knew, and not the inanimate object beneath him. The jumper spoke through clenched teeth. "Choppers can't fly in this."

"It'll calm down soon." But Max knew he was trying to convince himself. If they were lucky, the winds would calm sometime in the next two hours. That was a long time for Jackson.

A Missoula smoke jumper, Mark Salazar, held a mixture of Gatorade and water to Jackson's lips. Jackson sipped, regurgitated, sipped again.

Max wasn't sure when he'd ever seen anyone so brave.

"WHERE'S THE CAMERA?"

Max glanced up at the sound of the male voice, that of Jen's cohort. She was standing, already rejecting his instruction to stay where she was, and was peering around her back, trying to see her burns. Her jaw was stiff with pain, but she'd obviously made up her mind to deal with the situation. Which was how Max had remembered her.

Bob, the cameraman, was walking toward him and Jackson and Salazar.

Bob's face froze, suddenly gray, as he registered what had happened, why and how it had happened.

"Have a seat," Max told him because he looked faint. And he, himself, took a digital camera from inside his jumpsuit to photograph Jackson curled over the television camera, which he had chosen to protect with his own skin. "Want us to get that out from under you, John?"

"Thanks."

Bob's hands were there, ready to take the television camera. Max couldn't read his expression. Relief that his equipment had been saved? That what he'd recorded had been saved? Perhaps. But also revulsion toward the thing that Jackson had protected from fire at such a high personal cost.

The cameraman said, "Is there anything I can do?"

"Take care of yourself," Max answered.

Bob hoisted the camera to his shoulder, switched it on, began panning the blackened helispot.

Max's initial reaction—irritation—immediately gave way to pragmatism. The camera could provide fire information that would be useful to firefighters in the future—even to the extent of knowing what they risked.

"Jackson, want to be a film star?" he asked the burned jumper. "For all of us?"

Jackson knew what he meant. "Absolutely. That's why I did this."

Max tried to laugh, but it didn't quite come out. Still, Jackson's attitude was what would pull him through.

Smoke jumpers, Max sometimes thought, were born performers. The four of them at the helispot were, in the off-season, a civil-engineering professor, a paramedic, a Buddhist priest and a forest-service ranger. Tock was the Buddhist priest; Max the ranger, a ranger with solid qualifications in the world of firefighting and on his way to becoming a specialist in wildfire behavior.

Which made this burnover his own personal screw-up—one that might have repercussions in his career.

Not to mention that Jackson was burned.

Max had argued against this choice of helispot, but he was old enough and experienced enough with fire bureaucracies to know that the kind of argument that got heard was the kind he'd made the day before—refusal to cooperate. Today, he'd suggested to the hotshot superintendent who was second in command that the other side of the ridge could provide a safer helispot. The superintendent had argued—convincingly—that the alternative spot, Max's choice, was too far from crews. And in the end, Max had…agreed.

Those conversations, he knew, would be gone over again and again by fire investigators. Personal integrity would decide the outcome. When reputations were on the line, people often lied. Max had seen too much of it—and he was about to be in the middle of it again.

What mattered was that he'd agreed, and now Jackson was paying.

Max eyed the shelter that had been thrown aside, wishing for something that would remove the full weight of this disaster from his shoulders. But he'd already seen the cause of Jackson's misfortune. It was in Bob's hands, capturing Jackson's burns and all their blackened faces, witnessing the ash in the air.

Jackson should never have tried to protect the camera, should never have brought it into the shelter with him. If he hadn't, he would, in all likelihood, be leaving the helispot unburned. Granted, there had been room in the shelter. If two people could survive in a shelter—and this had happened many times—then one smoke jumper, with a camera could be fine. So Jackson must have paid more attention to protecting the camera than to holding down his shelter.

Yet this didn't make up for the bad choice of helispot, nor his—Max Rickman's—complicity in that selection. He had agreed. The end responsibility might not rest on his shoulders, but he felt his part in it.

He had been fighting wildfire for almost twenty years. Had lost a fiancée to fire, had known a total of six firefighters who'd died in the line of work.

Yet after none of those other events had he felt what he felt now.

That his life had been one way an hour and a half earlier and now was abruptly and completely changed.

This time, the blame was his.

JACKSON'S BURNS WOULD remain sterile for at least twenty-four hours, if they were not contaminated. The number one priority, as the fire had already burned their area and would not return, was to care for Jackson. Treat for shock and make sure that he drank. His airway seemed to be all right, not burned.

When Tock returned with water, Max and Salazar took turns offering Jackson canteen after canteen of water. Max knew he must make sure Jen was managing, as well, but her burns were not severe enough to cause excessive worry. Shock was still a possibility, but she seemed to be taking care of herself by concentrating on the filming of the helispot and shelters, all of which would have to be left as they were. He had photographed Jackson on top of the camera for the fire investigation. *To save yourself, Rickman?*

He would have done it any case. And there was no saving himself. It had always amazed him that at times like this supervisors were willing to lie to save their careers. This incident could negatively affect his future. Why *hadn't* he seen Jackson taking that camera into his shelter and stopped him?

Salazar, who worked as a paramedic when

not fighting fires, had taken over the care of Jackson, using the extremely limited first-aid kit that he carried on him at all times as his personal talisman. Fortunately for Jackson, the kit included Percocet. Salazar had offered Jen some, as well. She'd accepted ibuprofen, instead, which Max had watched her down with water from her canteen.

As the wind whipped over the helispot, Jen approached Max. "Any chance of seeing the incident commander?"

Max considered pointing out that her first appointment when they got off Silver Jack would be for critical-incident stress debriefing. But until that time, her mental health was his responsibility. Her determination to continue being Jen Delazzeri of Channel 4 might just be the best way for her to deal with what had just happened.

Bob, Max suspected, was going to have a lot more trouble in the long run. At some point, he'd given the camera to Jackson—or Jackson had taken it from him. Either way, Max knew that Bob might feel even more responsible for Jackson's burns than Max himself felt.

"Can he hike here, from where he is?" Jen asked, still on the trail of the IC.

"He's not going to. He's where they're fighting the fire."

Jen coughed, possibly from the smoke that was still in the air, and gazed at the slope above them. The wall of flame had torched everything in sight, and now the thick black smoke came from the horizon, beyond the rise.

Max couldn't blame Jen for what had happened to Jackson any more than he could have blamed her for Salma's death thirteen years before. Salma and Teresa had been working a different area, cutting line. Jen's presence in his shelter could not have been traded for Salma's. Maybe what had happened afterward between the two of them had been his way of acknowledging the fact that Salma's death hadn't been his fault, either.

"You shouldn't have been up here. Either of you." It came out anyhow. A mistake. Now was the time to support her, not to bring that trembling expression to her mouth. "But it's not your fault," he said. "It came from higher up."

Bob, who had been tending the camera, abruptly moved it aside and lurched toward a blackened stump at the edge of the area.

Max said, "Excuse me," to the brown eyes gazing out from that very exotic face, with its gorgeous bones—a face the camera must love. He went to check on the cameraman, who finished vomiting, straightened up and tentatively wiped his mouth.

"Sorry," Bob said, and his eyes were watery.

Max knew Jackson couldn't hear them. He put a hand on the cameraman's Nomex fire suit. "He knew better, Bob. You're not at fault."

"I would have taken it into my shelter, if he hadn't taken it."

"No, you wouldn't have, because none of us would have let you. Because we knew it wasn't safe. You have no blame in this."

Bob blinked through the haze. He was younger than Jen, maybe late twenties, with wire-rimmed glasses and a handsome, intelligent face. "Nobody's looked at Jen's burns."

"Actually, Salazar took a look at them. Drink some of that water in your canteen. And sit down. If you can't, if you feel like doing some work with that camera, you and I can take a walk together and get some film for the fire investigation."

"I'll come."

Max turned. He hadn't heard Jen behind him—only the wind.

"I'd like to hike down to where we first saw that smoke," she said, "to see where it started."

"I'd like to carry water," Bob said with a glance to where Jackson lay on his stomach, "for him."

"Tock's taken care of that. He went to the creek. But you'll help everybody by getting some of the information about this fire on film."

MAX RADIOED his division supervisor to let him know he'd be hiking with the two people from Channel 4 to film burned areas.

"Sure you want to do that?"

Max blinked, uncertain he'd heard correctly. Supervisors rarely raised objections in the form of questions.

"It will keep them busy until we can get them in critical-incident stress debriefing."

"Make sure they leave that television camera behind."

Did the supervisor know of the camera's role in Jackson's burns? No one had spoken of that over the airwaves, to Max's knowledge.

"Well, it's theirs," Max said. "I don't think they're going to leave it."

"Then, keep them on the helispot."

The supervisor, who did know of Jackson's burns, was covering his butt. Max considered feigning deafness, feigning problems with the communication. "The reporter got some second-degree burns. I don't think she'll want to go very far. We'll be concentrating on ecosystem changes. Their focus is world fire."

"Their focus is the news, Rickman."

Max couldn't believe what he was hearing. "I understand," he said—which did not mean compliance, he decided. It meant only that he registered the truth of the situation, which was that the supervisor wasn't keen to know what had gone wrong.

Max, on the other hand, did want to know. And wanted to make sure other fire personnel knew.

Signing off, he eyed Jen, who was noticing that some of her hair had been burned off.

"I don't remember it being on fire," she said. "I must have put it out and sort of blacked out the recollection."

The fire investigators would want her fire suit, as well, to see where it had failed when exposed to open flame. The gap had melted away a streak along the back of her thigh and her rear end. She had hung a bandanna from a tab to cover the gap.

Bob sank down on a burned stump. "Give me a minute."

Tock stalked over to them and offered Bob a canteen containing watered-down Gatorade.

The cameraman drank willingly.

"I'm going to go check out where I think this started," Max said.

"Going to take that?" Tock nodded at the television camera.

Bob said, "You know, I think I'll just stay here for a bit."

"Good plan," Max said. The elevation was a good 3000 feet higher than Denver. Bob seemed strong and fit, but he looked shaky after the ordeal of the fire.

Critical-incident stress debriefing. All of them needed it.

"I'd like to look at things," Jen said. "I have a tape recorder."

Max didn't object. He wasn't sure how he felt about her following, but it was better for him to be accompanied by someone—for a few reasons, some of them legal and bureau-cratic, protecting him by witnessing that he altered nothing of the scene—as if he could change anything meaningful. Someone experienced needed to remain at the helispot with Bob. Tock's lumbering, reassuring presence was already having a calming effect on the cameraman.

Bob said, "I thought I was dying. I've never been that scared in my life."

Yes, Tock was the person for this. The jumper took a seat on a burned log near Bob and sucked on his canteen. "It's terrifying," he agreed bluntly. "This is the worst burnover I've been in."

Max and Jen picked their way down from the helispot.

The helispot was at the edge of a steep, rocky cliff face that fell fifty or sixty feet to a wide gully below. Max found a path between blackened rocks, glancing behind him to make sure Jen was following safely. They discovered scorched junipers amid the rocks, but Max could see that high flames had reached up to the helispot, and winds had blown burning shrubbery in a fire whirl from the gully. "This is similar to what happened yesterday," he told her. "Yesterday, they were working on the edge of a ridge with a box canyon below, and the canyon acted as a chimney."

"Who picked the helispot?"

Well, that was getting to the heart of things.

"Division supervisor," he said. "And I agreed. This gully was relatively free of fuels."

But Jen had her tape recorder in her hand, even as she picked her way down the steep burned-over slope. Sweat had beaded all over her face, as he was sure it had on his. The sun beat down on them, and the wind threw ash and dust.

"It's like a moonscape," she said to the device in her hand. "But some vegetation actually escaped the blaze. I see incinerated piñons and junipers, yet here and there a low brush shows green beneath…" A pause. "A squirrel is burned here, frozen and black-ened in a kneeling, praying posture.

"Yet he is a reminder of humanity's first encounters with fire. When early people col-lected burnt animals after fires, undoubtedly they noted the improved flavor, which may have led to the practice of cooking meat."

Max stopped to take out his digital camera. These days, many firefighters carried them, because photographic evidence was so important to the record of fires. He snapped a photo down the slope, memorizing again the spot in the landscape from which the smoke had seemed to rise. He picked up a charred twig from the ground and snapped another photo, using the tip of the twig to mark the spot.

Max slid the cover so that the camera lens would retract. Wind whipped locks of curling black hair, or hair so dark brown that it seemed black, away from Jen's face. Impulsively, he opened the lens cap again, raised the camera and snapped a photo of Jen.

She smiled in response, that sudden smile, rare yet brilliant, that he remembered, and he clicked another shot.

"You're more beautiful than you were when we first met," he said. He marveled at the words as they came. He didn't say things like that.

Who would you say them to, Max?

There were women in his life, sometimes. Yet his lifestyle seemed to conflict with theirs. The ones with compatible lives were often so independent that a relationship wasn't a high priority.

That smile again.

And the smile was the same.

She said, "There will be a critical-incident debriefing, won't there?"

Despite the wind howling around them, Max heard her perfectly. "Oh, yes."

"Are you troubled about the fire investigation?"

"I'm troubled that Jackson got burned."

Jen felt herself to be an insensitive television reporter, asking the wrong questions. This was something she deliberately strived not to be. Off-camera time that wasn't spent with Elena was devoted to the study of martial arts; she spent time thinking about ethics. Always, she wanted to be better at her job.

Her fear, when the fire had come inside the shelter, was that her face would be burned.

And how close you were, Jennifer Delazzeri. Because her hair had been on fire, and she couldn't even remember it.

"It was a new fire. You know that, don't you?" he said.

"I didn't see how it could be anything else. Did it just ignite because of the heat of the day?"

He shrugged. "You know the fire triangle as well as I do."

Yes. Oxygen, fuel and heat—all must be

present for fire to exist. Fires were extinguished by eliminating one side of the triangle, one element. Cool it with retardant or water. Cut a fire line to clear brush. Smother it.

It took them only fifteen minutes to reach the spot where Max had seen the fire ignite. Below the spot were rocks and unburned piñon-juniper woodland.

Max photographed what he thought was the tree that must have produced the initial smoke—though how he could tell, Jen had no idea.

"May I observe the investigation?" she asked.

"I'm not the one to ask. I doubt they'll want a journalist there. Do you write at all?"

"You mean articles?"

"Yes."

"No. Not anymore. I have in the past."

"You seem to be doing well for yourself."

They turned to hike back. Jen could smell her burned hair as the wind whipped it round her face. "In my career, you mean?"

"Yes." He had been walking ahead of her, and he didn't pause as he said, "You don't have a family, do you?"

She didn't lie. She had great difficulty

saying anything untrue. But this, she thought, would be a good time to lie.

"I have a daughter. Elena."

"Pretty name."

Max asked no more. He simply wasn't that interested in her daughter, Jen supposed. The satisfaction of long-ago decisions suddenly turned bitter. No matter how many times she had considered finding him, telling him, she had been right to keep Elena's existence to herself. Because he wasn't interested.

And now she was old enough to appreciate that finding out you'd been right wasn't always satisfying.

CHAPTER THREE

THE CRITICAL-INCIDENT stress debriefing took place at the Super 8 Motel in Ridgway. For lack of a better place to gather, they sat around the glassed-in pool.

Jackson was in a hospital in Grand Junction, where he'd been air-lifted. But Jen had received medical attention at a local clinic and was able to attend.

Now, they sat around, the hardened smoke jumpers Max, Tock and Salazar, Bob and Jen, the division supervisor, whose name was Ted Stuart, a local psychologist whom Jen quickly decided was less than excellent, and an interagency fire investigator named Randy St. George. Jen was sure the investigator should be excluded from their debriefing.

Bob sat with his elbows on one of the circular white metal tabletops, his head in his hands, fingers pulling at his hair. The fire investigator, who seemed to sense he was something of an intruder, edged away from the rest of them and looked out the window at cars on the highway.

"He took the camera from you," Salazar said. "I saw it, Bob. He grabbed it—I would say *wrested* it—from you."

Tock answered, "I knew we weren't going to die. There wasn't enough fuel on the helispot. But it was loud. I can still hear it."

Max was quiet.

"Who saw the fire first?" Randy St. George turned from the window.

"I think I was the first to see the smoke," Max admitted. "It must have been smoldering for a while, though."

"What makes you say that?"

Jen tuned out. She had called Elena at dance camp, ten miles away in Ouray, to tell her daughter where she was staying and that she was okay. Because Elena was in class, Jen left a message. But she hadn't said, *Your father was with me.*

Elena knew that her father had been a wildland firefighter and a student when she was born. Jen had told her that Max had been in love with someone else, that the woman had died of burns sustained in a fire and that Jen had never told Elena's father of her existence.

Elena had only once asked why.

Because he was young and in love with another woman who had just died, and because he didn't love me.

Elena had not asked what that had to do with it—or why Max had made love with Jen if he was *in* love with someone else. But Jen had certainly asked herself those questions, and more, during the past twelve years. Many times, she'd considered trying to find Max and tell him about Elena. It was one thing not to consider Elena's rights or Max's when she herself was nineteen. But with each year that had passed, Jen found it more difficult to justify never telling Max that he had fathered a child.

Elena did not ask what he was like. Jen had said that Max saved her life during the Makal Canyon fire. She made him out to be a hero, a person from whom Elena could draw strength. A brave man.

No reason now to tell Elena that she had encountered Max again. Jen and Max were strangers; he was just someone she'd made love with long ago, when they'd both been other people.

She stole a look at him. His features were angular, rugged, movie-star handsome, charismatic. He had filled out, changing from the lanky young man he'd been into someone with solid muscles—and probably scars. As far as she could tell, his life was entirely about fire.

He'd become a fire addict. From hotshot to smoke jumper. He worked as a forest-service ranger in Leadville, but he'd also become something of an expert on fire behavior, she had learned.

Jen suspected that because it was a separate, new blaze that had overrun the helispot, Max and the others who had chosen the spot would be forgiven.

"I don't hear much from Jen," said the psychologist, a woman with straw-colored hair and an angular face, lined from years of sun exposure. "What happened in your shelter, Jen?"

She knew she was supposed to talk now, express her fear. And it was fear that had ultimately removed her from firefighting—

after what had happened to Salma. After she'd seen that people really did get burned fighting fires. That they died that way. She did not want to speak about fear, however; did not want anyone to know she'd ever been afraid.

"I don't remember when my hair caught fire," she said. "I remember that the flames were inside my shelter and that they burned through my pants before I could put them out. I had to hold down the shelter and put out the fire, and I couldn't do both. But I guess I did—I've been in a burnover before."

She felt, rather than saw, Max's cleft chin turn in her direction. His sudden attentiveness reminded her of Elena when her daughter was acting belligerent.

"When was that?" asked the psychologist, whose name Jen refused to remember.

"I was nineteen. I was a hotshot in California." Never saying that she had shared a shelter then; that the person who had shared his shelter with her was in the glassed-in pool area, too.

"Has anyone else been in this kind of situation before?" asked Ted Stuart, the division supervisor. "I know you have." A nod at Max.

"Not this bad," Tock said. "Not where anyone got hurt."

"It was my fault," Bob repeated. "I shouldn't have let him take the camera."

"He knew better," Ted shot back, overriding Bob's assertion.

"Do you want to talk about the previous experience you had, Jen?" asked the psychologist. "Any of you?"

Jen shook her head.

After the debriefing, Max walked beside Jen back to their hotel rooms. "I'll have to mention it in the fire investigation," he said. "That you're the person I shared a shelter with in Makal Canyon."

"How could that possibly be relevant?"

"It's not. But it will come out—whether I tell them or not."

"They won't say you were distracted by me, will they? I mean, people knew…" Jen let the sentence hang, undone.

People had known they were involved after the fire. Other Santa Inez Hotshots had seen it. And Teresa had known, of course. It only lasted about a week. A memorable week of not getting enough of each other, of sleeping and not sleeping in each other's nightmares, of clinging to each other in a variety of settings—on the beach, in the chaparral of the Santa Inez Mountains, in Max's truck, in bed. Frantic, desperate and fulfilling.

She still remembered how it had ended, and the sting had never gone away. Never.

"I don't know," Max said, as they reached the door of her room, "what will be said. Want to go into town and get some dinner?"

"No." The word came out sharply, too sharply. "I want to check my messages." *I want to talk to my daughter.*

"I can wait."

He was attractive, the most attractive man who had ever asked her to dinner—as a friend or otherwise—in her adult life.

But she could not forget how their weeklong affair had ended.

So? You're not going to sleep with him.

He had hurt her so badly, and he probably didn't even remember.

But more than a decade had passed. He must have changed. And didn't she owe it to Elena—if not Max—to find out how? Anyway, *she'd* changed.

"What are you thinking?"

She could not tell him the whole truth, not now. She settled on an earlier truth, instead. "I'm remembering when I was nineteen and in love with you, and you said, 'I don't love you. This is just about the fire. This is just because of the fire.'"

"Oh, God." His look was rueful, and he shook his head. "That sounds like something I would have said back then."

That was better than apologizing. These words meant that now he was a different person, a more mature person who wouldn't say anything so thoughtless and unfeeling.

As she had hoped.

"I'm sure it was true." She shrugged. "I just wasn't prepared for it." She had been a virgin before she slept with Max Rickman.

And for him it had been just about the fire—and just because of the fire.

He had loved another woman.

But he had been—and still was—very handsome. People who looked like that, she found, operated by different rules. While she knew she was attractive, she didn't have looks that would stop traffic or make people stare. But Max's striking features, the remarkable combination of brown eyes, blond hair and dark eyebrows and eyelashes, must have made women into a casual thing for him, easily seduced and therefore lacking challenge and of little particular importance. Maybe, she'd sometimes thought, she had even been interesting to him in comparison to other affairs he'd had because of the fire, because they'd shared a shelter, for example. But she'd been no more than another experience.

"Sure, I'll have dinner with you. I'll meet you in the lobby in fifteen minutes." That should give her time to return phone calls.

As she stepped into her room, she switched on her cell phone. Two messages.

One from station manager Gary Lowell. "Hey, Jen, I heard what happened. Glad everyone's okay." Jen thought of Bob and how he'd obviously been affected. "Tell Bob to send whatever you got. I'm calling him, too."

One from the Hotel Flora Vista in Ouray. From Elena at dance camp. "Hi, Mom. I'm glad you're okay. That's scary. Please call me."

Jen called the hotel and asked for Room Eleven. A girl whose voice Jen didn't recognize answered.

"Hi, this is Jen Delazzeri. Is Elena there?"

"Oh, yeah. Hang on." The girl on the phone sounded young, happy.

"Mom?"

"Hi, sweetie. Are you having fun?"

"Yes. What happened?"

Jen gave her daughter a brief description of what had happened.

"It doesn't sound like it was a very good place to land a helicopter," Elena remarked.

"No doubt that will come up in the fire investigation."

"Do you have to go back to the fire?"

"No."

Even if the station wants you to go back? Jen hadn't wanted to go anywhere near the fire in the first place, but someone was going to have to cover developments over the next few days for the news. She'd have to do it from the fire camp, which had been established on the local soccer field, just a block from the hotel.

"Are you sure?" asked Elena suspiciously.

"Yes." Now that she had said so, she would keep that promise. "Tell me about camp."

"It's cool. We do ballet in the morning, Afro-Haitian, jazz and improv in the afternoons." A pause. "Have you seen anyone you know?"

Jen thought her heart actually stopped for a moment. Elena wasn't asking about just anyone: Jen had been with wildland firefighters and Elena wanted to know if she had seen her—Elena's—father.

"Yes."

I don't know what to say, what to do. How can I say, "No, you can't meet your father because I'd still rather he not know that you exist?"

"I have to go, because I'm having dinner with one of the smoke jumpers. I love you."

JEN HAD WORN a draped silk outfit in a deep purple to the debriefing. She was here in a professional capacity and she was not about to relax her professional look. Because she had so much hair, the part that had been burned did not present a huge problem. She'd done nothing but shampoo it, trying to get the smells of the fire off her body and out of her mind. She'd failed to accomplish either, however.

Briefly she scrutinized her reflection before leaving the room, her black handbag slung over her shoulder. She hurried down to the lobby.

Max, still wearing the off-white canvas pants he'd had on at the debriefing, had exchanged a black button-down shirt for his red Leadville smoke jumper T-shirt. He offered her a new bottle of spring water as he stood up to meet her. "You need to keep drinking," he said.

Because of her burns.

"Up to walking?" he asked.

"Much better," she admitted, "than sitting in a car." Sitting, in general, took particular care because of her burns. The local emergency physician had prescribed painkillers, in case she had trouble sleeping, but so far she'd stuck to ibuprofen.

They left the hotel, walked down to a corner gas station and crossed the highway at the traffic light.

"Mexican, Chinese or steaks?"

"I'm a vegetarian."

"Ah. Well, the question is pretty much the same."

"Mexican?"

"You're on, but you should stay away from the margaritas."

Again, because of the burns. As they walked past the fairgrounds and down a side street, Jen was almost certain she'd be forced to take the prescription pain relief she'd been given in order to sleep that night.

"You never stop being a firefighter, do you," she said, as she sipped from her water bottle. "I mean, telling me to drink water, stay away from alcohol."

"True. Well, I'm a ranger in my other life. I spend a lot of time looking out for people and protecting natural resources. Sorry—it's hard to shut off the caregiver thing."

"I wasn't complaining. Just observing."

There was a wait at the restaurant. Still, Jen didn't want to sit, so they walked onto the patio and stood, looking at the high desert plants illuminated by low southwestern-style lanterns. The air was full of smoke. No escaping it, anywhere.

"What did they ever find out," she asked, "about Makal Canyon? The fire investigation." They'd both had to deal with those memories, had to face them. Max was still in the profession, so he must know what had been determined about the fire.

"Not much."

She heard the dissatisfaction in his deep voice.

"The South Canyon fire had happened a couple of weeks earlier, and that was considered the debacle of the year. And so the Makal Canyon investigation was hurried, and there were definite errors in the report."

"They got things wrong?"

"A couple of things, at least. They missed the absence of a lookout on the east flank, for one thing. And I'm pretty sure someone widened a bulldozer line two days after, to make it look sufficient. And they blamed Salma, too."

"For what?"

He hesitated, seemed to be choosing his words carefully. "It's a pity you don't write and that investigative journalism isn't your thing."

"I *can* write, and I like film as a medium. Are you saying there was some cover-up about Makal Canyon?" Her pulse quickened. This wasn't the kind of thing she did. "Anyhow," she said, "you can write, can't you?"

He nodded but didn't answer her question about a cover-up.

"Max?" called someone from the doorway.

It was the hostess, who had come to seat them.

"Can I get you something to drink?" she asked as Jen and Max sat down.

"I'm fine," Jen told the hostess. But she wasn't; sitting was hell.

"Just water, for both of us." As the woman left, Max noticed Jen's discomfort. Abruptly, he stood. "I'll be right back."

He went toward the kitchen and returned several minutes later with some clean folded towels. "See if you can use these to keep the pressure off those burns. You can prop yourself up on other parts of your body."

"Right," she agreed, and arranged the towels on her seat. "Better."

With water and chips in front of them, Max asked, "If there was some kind of a cover-up with Makal Canyon, are you interested? If we could make a film about the fire? Interview survivors—and fire managers. Hunt down the principals."

"What do you know about filmmaking?" She sounded waspish, but she didn't much care.

"Half my undergraduate work was in film studies. It's not much, I know, but it's something. I've also helped make a training film for wildland firefighters."

Jen considered. "It's still impractical. I'd have to support myself—" *and our daughter* "—in the interim. Also, finding people, witnesses, survivors, former supervisors, isn't always easy."

"Well, Teresa was there," he said. "Presumably, you know your own sister's address."

Teresa? *Interview survivors…*

But it was hard to call Teresa a survivor. Or rather, she'd survived so much *more* than the fire. There were the dead, including Salma.

And the other dead.

The living dead.

That's not fair, Jen. You know perfectly well that Teresa's far better off than if she'd died, that her life, her existence, has value.

"You're not talking," Max observed.

Could she tell him that Teresa *wasn't* okay?

No, actually she couldn't. Teresa was sensitive, and sometimes hypersensitive, about her mental health issues, not wanting anyone to know about them. But it was hardly a secret to anyone who interacted with Teresa.

And saying that it had been caused entirely

by the fire was untrue. Teresa's psychiatrist believed it was also at least partly hereditary. Though the trauma, he acknowledged, couldn't have helped.

"Teresa won't take part," Jen said.

"Why not?"

"She doesn't like…the limelight."

He raised his eyebrows.

Teresa *had* liked the limelight. Teresa had believed herself brilliant and she had been proud of that brilliance. Her plan had been to specialize in burn treatment. But the plan had gone awry.

"What's she doing?"

Jen eyed him. His steady gaze read more than she told. She felt herself being read, felt exposed telepathically. Well, she could keep up the charade. Because she could say a great deal more and neither lie nor betray her sister. "Going to school."

"Did she finish medical school?"

Ah, to the crux. "No."

Two things he did seem to pick up—that Jen didn't want to discuss her sister, and that something was wrong.

He would assume, she thought, that the fire had been the catalyst for all possible disasters. Perhaps it had led to Teresa's change, of course; the disappointment of her dreams.

"Wouldn't you like to know," he asked, "what really happened?"

"It's your quest," she said. "I mean, *you're* the one with the interest, not me." But that wasn't true. Her survivor's guilt after Makal Canyon had been minimal, but it hadn't stopped what she'd felt on Teresa's behalf. In hindsight, it had been obvious that the west flank crew, of which Teresa and Salma had been a part, should never have been where it was, that the safety zone was less safe than it should have been and that the firefighters had been given inadequate air support before the blowup. As Max had pointed out, similar things had happened earlier that summer in Colorado.

But Jen hadn't had the leisure to brood about what had gone wrong. Six weeks after the fire, she'd discovered she was going to have a child. And by then Max Rickman was out of the picture. She was pregnant and alone.

Now he wanted her to look into the Makal Canyon fire that had killed his fiancée?

She wouldn't do it—do something that would bring the two of them into extended contact—and perhaps bring him and Elena to each other's attention.

Is it your right, Jen, to make that call? Didn't she ask you on the phone tonight if you'd run into any old acquaintances?

Our life is simple now.

But it wasn't, really. There was nothing simple about their all-female household, directed by a sometimes unstable matriarch and inhabited by Jen's equally unstable sister. It was Jen's family, but there was no pretending that any of its attributes could compensate Elena for the absence of a father. Didn't Jen owe it to her daughter to at least confess the truth to Max; to at least find out if he was interested in meeting Elena, getting to know her, even assuming some of his parental duties?

Part of her screamed, *Don't do it! Don't tell him! You won't be able to take it back.*

But it was for Elena—she must do this for Elena. Thirteen years ago it had mattered that Max didn't love her; that he was mourning Salma. Yet now, she was older, and she could tell him the truth. She didn't need his financial or emotional support. She had raised Elena alone up to this point, and she could certainly go on alone. Her revelation would be no threat to him.

And she was equal to dealing with the unlikely possibility that he would be angry. After all, why should he be? He hadn't loved her and had told her so. If she'd told him that she was pregnant, who knew how he would have reacted?

She thought this over, as he let the subject of Makal Canyon drop and picked up his menu. She followed suit, and it wasn't until their waitress had come and taken their orders that Jen spoke to Max again.

"Max, I have something to tell you, something I never intended…" She took a sip of water.

"Drink more," he said, seeming not to have heard. "I'm considering you under my care this evening. In addition to eating a good meal, you need to drink plenty of water."

"Yes. Max, the thing is that Elena…"

"Elena?"

Maybe she would keep it to herself.

"My daughter. She's twelve. She's…"

All of a sudden, his look turned sharp, aware. He waited, staring, hawklike.

"You're her biological…natural…father."

CHAPTER FOUR

MAX SAID, "Why are you telling me this?" then wished he could call back the question.

"If it makes you happier, forget that I did." Jen drank more water and helped herself to some chips.

Her manner had become almost indifferent, but only on the surface. She was brusque, concerned with rearranging herself slightly on her stack of folded towels, confident in her own person. This was all visible. Less apparent was whatever his question had actually made her feel.

"I told you," she said, "because it seemed decent to do so."

"'Decent' would have been telling me thirteen years ago when you found out you were pregnant."

"You didn't love me. We only ended up together because of the fire. You moved on to other things, mourning Salma, and I figured the pregnancy was my responsibility. I didn't use birth control."

"Obviously, neither did I." And he'd known she was a virgin.

"Well, I've found life goes more smoothly for everyone if I take responsibility for my actions," Jen said, lifting her chin and smiling. Not the sudden radiant smile that showed her teeth, that made anyone who saw it smile back. A closed smile. It seemed peaceful, accepting—and utterly unlike the Jen he knew. Granted, Max didn't know about her life with her—their—daughter, but he knew her essence. They had been friends.

I don't want children.

He had decided *not* to have children—and fairly soon after his affair with Jen. He'd begun to use condoms. He'd even considered having a vasectomy until a lover told him that she never had sex without condoms even with men who'd had vasectomies, because as far as she was concerned, there were just too many sexually transmitted diseases around. He'd become fastidious in this regard.

But before that he had fathered a child with Jen Delazzeri.

Yet he still wanted to say, in some kind of accusing way, *I don't want children.*

It didn't sound as though she wanted help with her—their—daughter. Yet now this child was a fact.

She changed things.

Max knew he'd have to think, spend time thinking, before he decided what to do.

"We should," he said, grasping for something to say, "exchange permanent contact information."

Jen opened her handbag and, from her wallet, produced a business card.

I have a child. He tried to say something positive, to thank her, perhaps, for raising his child. He could have asked to see a photo. But none of those thoughts occurred. "You should have told me when it happened." Another recrimination. All he seemed able to utter.

I have a daughter.

"I'm just shocked," he managed to say, when she didn't answer. "I'm not handling this well."

"And I'm asking nothing of you," she said. "I never expected to see you again, truthfully. Not after a certain point.

"I'm telling you now because here you are…." Her voice drifted off.

Max stepped back, held the news he'd just received at a distance. He thought about the smoke jumper he was, carefully distant from ties of love, suspicious of commitment, which was—somewhere in his heart—associated with loss.

Jen asked for no commitment. Yet the sense of commitment was there now.

Feeling helpless, he said, "I work in fire, Jen. That's the choice I've made. I like it. But as long as I'm a smoke jumper, I can't deal with children." Because smoke jumpers were away from home too much. Because their work was too dangerous. Because to have children was to belong to them and, so, to have to take care of himself… Not the way he *did* take care of himself—but like someone, or something, that belonged to someone else.

But as soon as he'd spoken, he saw something happening in her eyes. A veil coming down, hiding her emotions, hiding the hurt.

Did he have obligation in this situation? "Is my name on her birth certificate?"

"Of course not." She sounded and looked

disdainful. "Did you think I was going to come after you for child support?"

"I don't care about that. I would help. But I don't want her to know me."

"I don't *want* anything from you," she said, and this time she sounded disgusted. "I didn't tell you about Elena so that you would *do* something. Does she want to know her father? Yes." That was why Jen had told him the truth after all this time.

"Do I want her to know you?" She shrugged. "If you and Elena both wanted that, I would say, 'Sure, go ahead.' But you're pretty clear that you *don't* want that. So…my life is easier."

Had she intended to wound him with her indifference? He *wasn't* wounded. Just curious. "What have you told her about her father?"

"That we were hotshots together."

"Hasn't Teresa put two and two together?"

"Teresa's always known the truth. But she wouldn't tell Elena."

Still observing himself from the outside, Max surmised that his own behavior marked him as someone who maybe should not be told by a woman that she had conceived a child with him. He'd responded with selfishness and insensitivity and he knew it.

"And you said she wants to know her father? Elena?" He tried out the name.

"Yes."

He remembered this straightforward honesty. It was trademark Jennifer Delazzeri. She'd never been given to scenes, for instance. She remained, to this day, one of the most levelheaded lovers in his life. She said what she thought and felt without fanfare and without deception.

He *had* treated her insensitively, and she'd said so. Not then, but today.

He liked her. There was nothing *not* to like.

Except that now he knew he was a father, and he didn't know any positive way to react because it wasn't what he'd planned for himself.

I can't. I just can't be a father to someone. He was a father biologically, but he couldn't meet this daughter he and Jen had somehow produced; couldn't let her know him, come to depend upon him. And not only because he expected to die fighting fires—which he didn't. He hoped to move up through the hierarchy of firefighting strategists to take charge of the biggest blazes, always learning more about the best ways to manage wildfire. Smoke jumping was for now, and it was just a rung on the ladder.

I don't want anything from you, she had said.

He believed her. If she wanted something from him, she'd have come out and said so. She wasn't a schemer.

"Do you want me to know her?" he asked.

"I already answered that."

He supposed she had.

"In any case," she said, "I think your answer puts paid to my helping you with a documentary on Makal Canyon. It's not a sure thing that Elena would put two and two together, but she might. And if she asks me outright if you're her father, I won't lie to her."

He could see the wisdom of that.

Strange, before Jen had sprung this on him—and he couldn't stop himself from framing her announcement in that accusatory way—he'd wanted badly to return to Makal Canyon *with her.* He needed others who'd been there, others who'd experienced that fire, that day, to be with him, to look back with him.

But her news complicated everything.

Why hadn't they used birth control?

What does it matter now, though? She doesn't want anything from you.

But he couldn't forget. Now, he had a daughter and he *knew* he had a daughter. His life was different.

He was ashamed that Jen or any human being alive should see this side of him, should see him *not* welcome the news that he was a father. What would *his* father say if he knew of Max's reaction?

Max preferred not to consider that. His father had always taken parenthood seriously. When Max's mother had been diagnosed with cancer, when Max was twelve and his sister thirteen, his dad, an orthopedic surgeon, had expanded his already active roles as soccer coach, faithful attendant at plays and homework tutor to do the carpooling and cooking. Six years later, Max's mother had died, and his father had never turned his back on his role as husband and father.

A paragon.

And I'm headed for the title of Deadbeat Dad of the Year.

Why?

Why was that the choice he wanted to make, now that he was confronted with the existence of a child of his own?

"Remind me how old she is," he said, doing the math one more time.

"Twelve. She was born April nineteenth."

He blinked. "That's my birthday."

"I know."

Max wondered what, if anything, this meant. He couldn't remember Jen's birthday, if he'd ever known it.

But he *had* known it. It had come sometime during the week after the fire. He'd bought her flowers and dinner. Nothing permanent. Nothing *was* permanent. "Yours," he said finally, "is at the end of July."

"The twenty-sixth."

She appeared not to care much about her birthday—or his.

The waitress brought their food, and Jen began to eat. Elegantly, simply.

Max changed the subject. "Jen, *would* you want to work on a documentary on Makal Canyon? Would you at least be willing to go back with me, to do some research, to hunt down supervisors?"

"I have a job."

"Could you take a leave of absence?"

Jen shook her head, thinking that if she left the station, it would be for good. She'd been considering a move, perhaps even to a station in another part of Colorado, but that didn't mean she could afford to go without paid work while investigating the Makal Canyon fire.

Also, she was reluctant to step away from the job she had without rising in her career. Making a documentary about a little-known wildfire that had happened more than ten years ago and completely overshadowed by fourteen deaths on Storm King Mountain did not seem like the smartest move. More like a distraction from everything that mattered to her.

She supposed Max's reaction to the news of Elena didn't surprise her, but it did disappoint her. He was still a handsome man, of course, but any attraction she'd once felt had evaporated when she'd seen how he felt about her daughter—biologically, also his. His presence as a firefighter that afternoon had been powerful. His presence as a man with other values was weak, clearly. He'd become a smoke jumper probably for the thrill, the pleasures of the work; he was *about* being a smoke jumper.

In her mind she consigned him to a shelf with other men "of that type." She had a child and a family who relied on her. And as for Max, he wanted no ties of any kind, not even to his own daughter.

Jen shifted on the folded towels and considered standing up for a moment or taking a pill for the pain.

"What if I paid you?"

She stared at Max, and couldn't stop herself from half laughing. "How could you do that?"

"I have some money."

"You don't have the kind of money I make," she told him flatly.

"I remember this about you."

"What?" she demanded.

"You just say what you think."

"No, I don't. It doesn't work in television." *And I definitely haven't said everything I think about you.*

He laughed then. And glanced away from the table, then looked back to her. His jaw was tense, frozen in motion.

He was still reacting to her revelation.

Was his conscience kicking into gear? Jen didn't trouble herself over the point. At the moment, she didn't like him much—Elena was better off without him.

She said, "The answer on Makal Canyon is no."

"Because I don't want to be a father."

You are a father, damn it.

"For many reasons," she said.

"I don't know what I feel yet, Jen. Let alone what I should do. I've only known for fifteen minutes that you and I made a child together and that now she walks the earth. Give me a little time before you consign me to your permanent list of fiends."

"It's easier for me if you just stay away," she said sharply. "I told you for Elena's sake, to give her a chance if you wanted to know her. But you don't and…"

"I'm not sure about that." Max jerked his head back as he spoke, as though he'd said something regrettable.

"You're not going to involve my daughter in some emotional circus just because you want me to help you investigate the death of your fiancée." Now, Jen wished she hadn't spoken. What on earth had made her phrase the objection that way? But she couldn't stop trying to put the words right. "I just mean, it's not mature to do that to Elena. She doesn't need to meet some person who doesn't care about her, just so she can put a face to her biological father."

"How do you know?"

Jen nearly stood and left the restaurant then. Her burns were stinging, the pain suddenly intense. And Max had just said that he didn't care about Elena, but that it might be helpful for Elena to meet him anyhow. How could he think Jen would expose her daughter to that kind of pain? "Let's just say," she replied, "that I know."

"You're in pain."

"Of course I'm in pain," she hissed, and then she did stand up, grabbing up her purse. "But don't think it has anything to do with you."

MAX WISHED he hadn't gotten a hotel room for the night; wished he'd gone back down to the fairgrounds to be with the other firefighters. But after the second catastrophe in two days, he was off this fire for an enforced—and he hoped brief—period. Getting a hotel room, relaxing, had seemed the intelligent thing to do.

Now he lay in an alien environment, suddenly alien to himself as well, as if he'd become someone else in the past few hours.

Since Jackson had been burned, Max supposed he *had* become someone else. He was responsible for serious injuries to another jumper—and he was a father. As for the first thing, he wished it was untrue. And as for the second…

Why didn't I know?

As if the fact of conceiving a child with Jen should have been known to him at the moment.

The circumstances…

Not even Jen really understood the reasons he'd made love to her again and again and again.

Now he sat on the edge of the large empty bed with the generic polyester spread, the mirror reflecting an unshaven, half-dressed man, not even a smoke jumper now.

Tock had taken a room down the hall, and Max considered rousing him. It was only eleven and Tock would still be awake. They could talk—about Jackson—about the choice of helispot.

But it wasn't Jackson Max wanted to see.

He grabbed his shirt and withdrew the business card he'd tucked in the breast pocket.

It was late, but could she be sleeping?

Her burns… She would have taken her pain medication. If she had managed to fall asleep, he should leave her alone.

On the other hand, if she was awake…

SHE WATCHED HERSELF on the eleven o'clock news and had her first glimpse of the incident commander as he was interviewed by someone from Channel 7. How had Bill Black gotten to the IC? Not by being caught in a burnover.

Her cell phone rang, playing Ravel's "Bolero."

She opened it to check the number.

This hotel.

There was only one person it could be.

She answered.

"How is the burn?"

"I'm floating. Percocet."

"Ah. Could I come see you?"

She considered her attire. A long T-shirt

Teresa had given her, emblazoned with the words, *I haven't been the same since that house fell on my sister.*

She should say no.

Or should she say yes?

To Makal Canyon. To walking over burned ground.

"You can come down," she said.

She grabbed the loose raw silk pants that she'd found the most bearable against her injury.

Then she went to her door. He was already there, in the pants he'd worn to dinner, with a faded forest service T-shirt bearing an image of Smokey Bear and the words ONLY YOU.

She said, "You know, of course, that he was a real bear. A cub whose mother was killed in a forest fire."

"I do know this."

Jen tried to remember the things she'd felt in the restaurant, but the pain medication made it impossible for her to summon that anger. Now, things were different. Elena slept safely in Ouray, happy at her dance camp, unaware that her father wished she didn't exist—or at least wished he didn't know of her existence.

He shut the door behind himself and sat on one of the two queen-sized beds in her room, gazing at the television screen and watching the flames of the Silver Jack fire.

"Did you know those smoke jumpers well?" she asked.

"No. One was a rookie. We're not as close-knit as the hotshots were."

Jen remembered just how close they had been, the Santa Inez Hotshots. Like family.

Max kept his face turned toward to the TV screen.

Jen stepped past him and lay facedown on the other bed.

He said, without looking at her, "Salma was pregnant."

Jen heard. Thought. Tried to understand what this meant. Did this have something to do with his not wanting children? Was the pregnancy why he and Salma had planned to marry?

She could see only his profile. There was nothing more to read.

"Do you have a picture of her?" he asked.
Elena.

"Why? What does Salma's having been pregnant have to do with it?" she wanted to know. Though the pain relief was effective, she could feel a part of her mind clearing.

"Nothing, Jen. It's just one of the things that's made me... How I've become." He searched for his words in the pauses.

Jen didn't want to hear any more of Max's views on fatherhood, so she stood up, retrieved her purse, found her wallet, and took out the picture of Elena she carried, a school photo from the previous fall.

Her daughter was blond, like Max.

She looked like the two of them, although people said she had Jen's smile.

Max took the photo from Jen and stared at it.

Elena had braces, but still he knew her mouth. He saw himself in the shape of her eyes and her nose. "How tall is she?" he asked.

"About five-foot-eight. Taller than me."

"She's pretty."

"Yes," Jen agreed.

She's my daughter.

Max felt himself change again. He said, "I was ambivalent about the baby. But...I was raised a certain way. I loved Salma and I wanted to marry her."

"But you were young," Jen said distantly, remembering herself, pregnant with Elena. Young. Knowing that her life would change, would be mapped by events she hadn't foreseen. Knowing that she would be a mother at nineteen.

"I was blown away that she was pregnant. It seemed incredible that she and I had created a life between us."

"I really don't want to hear this." The statement was unlike her—callous. Teresa had watched Salma die. Had Teresa known Salma was pregnant? If so, she'd never said.

Jen wanted to call her sister, no matter the hour, and find out what Salma had told her in the burn unit.

Max stared at her. Dispassionate; maybe wondering why she had any feelings at all about Salma's pregnancy so long ago.

You are thick, she thought. "Look," she said, "don't delude yourself. You have ceased to be much of a factor in any of it now, but at the time I was… Well, I suppose, in love with you.

"You were in love with Salma, who had just died. Now, you're telling me Salma was pregnant when she died. I was pregnant and

I didn't die. The 'baby' is twelve years old and dancing in Ouray this week."

Max shot another look at her.

Jen cursed the Percocet. Why had she chosen those words? Did she want Max to know Elena was that close, that he could see her if he liked? Did she believe that if he saw her his feelings would change?

Yes, she believed that. But still she wished she hadn't told him Elena was nearby.

"She's in Ouray?"

"Now you want to see her? Meet her?"

"I think so."

Jen considered. In a way, it was what she'd set out to achieve. But Max's ambivalence had changed things.

Or had it?

"This isn't something I can figure out tonight," she said. "Let me sleep on it. Maybe you should, too. And then I'll ask Elena if she wants to meet you. I strongly suspect she does."

"What does she like to do?" he asked.

"She likes to dance."

"No surprise." He smiled, but the smile was uneasy, uncommitted. "What kind of dance?"

"Modern dance and ballet. She likes

theater, too. Actually, she wants to apply to the performing arts high school in Denver so she can pursue all these things."

He nodded, distractedly watching a commercial for identity-theft protection.

After a moment he asked, "What's her whole name?"

"Elena Allegria Delazzeri."

Max wondered how he would ever sleep. "Do you have another copy of this photo?"

"You can have that one," she said. Her initial anger began to fade.

Max's cell phone chimed, and he opened it to see who was calling. Tock.

"Hey," he said, answering.

"Want to go back on the fire line?"

Yes, was the easy answer. Maybe fighting fire could help him to forget what Jen had told him.

But, no, Salma and the baby she had carried were part of every fire. Jen was, too.

"They aren't going to let us," he told Tock.

"Wrong. They're too short-handed. Alex just called."

Their foreman.

"He said to show up at the fairgrounds at six, if we're willing."

Max saw Jen rest her head on her arms. "I'll be there," he said.

After hanging up, he told her, "I'm back on the fire. What are you doing tomorrow?"

Her head lifted. "They're letting you go back up there?"

"Not enough personnel."

"Will you be all right?"

He didn't know what he'd expected from her. At first, he'd wondered if she would show her journalist side, seeking information about decisions that had been made, ready to assign blame for past and future events. Instead, she spoke as a friend.

He remembered, from a time far away, the closeness of the Santa Inez Hotshots. He shared a closeness with other jumpers, too, and he supposed that was part of what he loved about firefighting.

"Yes," he said, studying her. "This isn't related to your… To…to Elena. What about going back to Makal Canyon?"

"Why do *you* want to go back?" she asked. "Is this about Salma?"

"In part. But the whole picture wasn't right. I've got a graduate degree in fire science, Jen. Fires are what I do with my life and Makal Canyon is part of the reason I've chosen this work. I understand things better, now. I want to know what went wrong there."

Jen thought about the books by Norman and John Maclean, which she had read, revisiting Mann Gulch and Storm King. But Max wanted to put his findings on film.

"Find members of the crew?" she asked. "Supervisors? But, Max, it's not like the subject has that wide an audience. One person died—Salma. It's not like Storm King, where the public is going to be overwhelmed and outraged. It happened a long time ago."

"It will have an audience among people who fight wildfire."

"What will happen if you find that the decisions of a certain person were responsible?"

"Decisions of a certain person *were* responsible."

Jen did not ask who. Richard Grass had been superintendent of the Santa Inez Hotshots. Richard, who had been like a Zen master; who had practiced t'ai chi chuan every day of his life. Who had been so focused—whom they had idolized, all of them. It was Richard whom Max held responsible.

Strange that Jen, who'd become so involved in martial arts herself, rarely thought of Richard.

"I think you should let it go," she said.

"He's still in fire, Jen."

Max's sudden intensity far outweighed any emotion he had shown at the news that he had a twelve-year-old daughter.

"He made a *mistake*."

"A similar mistake to the one made at Storm King. He's never been held accountable."

"You think he doesn't hold himself accountable?"

"Please," Max said. "Do this with me."

He had moved off the one bed and now he crouched beside the other, his face level with hers.

"Why me?" She was not susceptible to feelings for a Max who used to be, the long-ago lover she'd cared for. She had become a different woman and he was a different man. Yes, she dated. She'd even had two lovers since Max. The first hadn't lasted long; she'd ended it. The second... Well, she'd been relieved when he moved away.

Her path? Career was part of it, although not in an overly ambitious way. Elena was ambitious; Elena wanted to dance professionally, choreograph, have a school and ultimately a company of her own; and Jen doubted that ambition would change. In some twelve-year-olds who loved to dance, yes. But not in her daughter. And most of Elena's decisions, even at twelve, were made with that single goal in mind.

"Jen," he said, "we were together. You and I shared a shelter in that fire. You're a journalist. Why anyone else? Why would I want anyone but you to help me with this?"

Today they'd been together again. Not sharing a shelter, yet with that same fearing-for-their-lives intimacy. "And my sister was with Salma," Jen added.

"Tell me what Teresa is up to."

Ah. There it was. No opportunity to get away from it. "She has mental health problems."

"From the fire?"

"No. Partly… No one really knows. It's in the family, though."

"What precisely?"

"My mother's father was schizophrenic."

He waited, showing no reaction.

"My mother… Well, her issues are more situational. My parents divorced when I was three. And my mother… Let's say she tended to create drama where none was necessary."

Max still said nothing.

"As for Teresa, well, she gets depressed. It's more than that. We all live together, my mother, Teresa, Elena and me. My mother and I bought the place together."

"Does she work—your mother?"

"She's retired now. She was a nurse practitioner."

"So her problems didn't keep her from holding down a job."

"No. She always worked." Jen tried to imagine successfully explaining her mother to Max but she couldn't work it out. Her fear, a fear she'd always held, was that her mother's behavior would rub off on her. Not that her mother was a bad mother. On the contrary, Robin Delazzeri had always cared for her children diligently, which was one of the reasons she'd always looked so good to the courts.

And there'd always been courts.

There had always been drama.

It filled Jen with shame and also anger when she remembered. Gino Delazzeri had been no prince. The fisherman son of Irish and Italian immigrants, he'd drunk more than was good for him or anyone close to him.

He'd cheated on his second wife, just as he had on the first. He'd taken his daughters to bars and taught them to shoot pool and let them sip the foam off his beer. He'd brought them to the Monterey docks to see the commercial fishing vessels that were his home when he was away. He'd talked about the sea; told stories of the waves, of drownings, of sharks, of storms.

His daughters had loved him and they'd wanted to see him.

But by the time Jen was eleven, higher wages elsewhere and her mother had finally driven Gino away, to Gulf Coast ports and then back to his East Coast roots. Jen and Teresa hadn't blamed him.

They'd watched their mother lie—not just lie but *perform*—to keep him away from them. And instead of enjoying a week in Hawaii or Squaw Valley or Disneyland with their dad, they'd found themselves bustled to women's shelters in the middle of the night.

They'd been baffled. Though they'd sometimes seen their dad throw things in exasperation, they'd never seen him so much as touch their mother in anger. He'd never laid a hand on either of them.

Whenever they'd seen him, they'd run to him with delight. Jen still remembered how her dad had swung her up onto his shoulders and how she'd liked being able to see, knowing that she could suddenly be the tallest person in a crowd.

The other women in the shelters often had bruises and broken bones, and most of all, terrified expressions. And their mother had been able to look terrified, as well. But as far as Jen knew, there'd never been any real reason for terror.

Jen had begun to put two and two together around the age of seven, the first time she'd heard her mother say to her father, over the phone, "I'd like to go to Hawaii, too. Why don't you just take me along?" Eventually she'd realized that her mother was still in love with her father.

Now she understood that her mother's reaction to not being loved by her husband had been to deprive him of his daughters. She was determined to punish him for rejecting her.

Jen had grown up aware of her mother's deceit, and one of her greatest fears, from the time she'd realized just how appalling her mother's behavior was, had been that people would think she was like her, capable of the same sorts of lies.

Because she wasn't like that, tried her hardest *not* to be like that.

And maybe it was because her own mother had done everything in her power to keep Jen from knowing Jen's dad, that Jen especially wanted Elena to know Max. He seemed to feel that his work was too dangerous to allow him to have a family. But Jen knew that didn't matter. It was more important for a child to know his or her father.

For herself, the chance for more hours with her father was gone, because he'd died.

Now, considering her seesawing emotions in the face of Max's ambivalence about meeting Elena, Jen felt slightly ashamed. Part of her responsibility as Elena's mother was to help facilitate her daughter's relationship with her father—not impede that relationship. Hadn't she learned that the hard way herself?

She said to Max, "Teresa…I guess she's a bit borderline, maybe. I don't know. My mother has a flair for drama, and so does my sister. She's had some bad experiences with men. She'll see something on television and have a meltdown.

"She can't really hold down a job. I mean, I don't think she's consciously trying to get attention or anything like that. It's just… Some people have a higher tolerance for stressful circumstances than other people do."

"Being next to Salma when she was burned is high on a list of stressful circumstances."

Suddenly, Jen could hear Jackson's screams again.

Could feel her own burns.

And these things were unpleasant, but she had taught herself not to show fear. Because—for her—a person who showed fear was like Robin Delazzeri. Or rather, because Jen was Robin's daughter, if she showed fear people would think she was like her mother.

She would think she was like her mother; she would think she was showing fear because it might earn her attention and sympathy.

And Jen didn't want that kind of attention or that kind of sympathy. She wanted the inner integrity of knowing that she didn't lie, deceive or create scenarios for her own ends.

"So," Max said, "you want to protect Teresa from revisiting Makal Canyon."

"Yes." The hesitation, the indecision, came through. "I don't know, Max. Maybe it would be good for her. But I won't pressure her. You have to know that. If you try…"

"I won't," he interrupted. "Her input isn't necessary. There are other survivors—others who were with them on the west flank."

Jen nodded. Max stood, then sat down again on the other bed, facing her but clearly lost in plans of his own. Thinking about returning to the fire the next day, she imagined, or about making a documentary on the Makal Canyon fire.

He said, "I want to know Elena. I want to be a dad to her."

Jen looked at him. "Do you mean you want that? Or do you mean you *want* to want it?"

"Both."

An honest answer, and honesty was the quality she prized above all others.

"When will you be off this fire?"

"I'll probably be up there till it's under control."

Days.

"Elena has five more days at dance camp."

"If I can't meet her here," he said, "I'll come to Denver. Or you two can come to Leadville. And if you work with me on investigating Makal Canyon, I imagine I'll be seeing a lot of her."

"She needs to go back to school in the fall," Jen warned. "And I haven't said yes."

"I know." He touched her hand where it lay on the spread; covered her hand.

She didn't know what it meant, that touch. But she realized she both feared and wanted whatever it was.

CHAPTER FIVE

ELENA DELAZZERI *DID* WANT to meet her father, the smoke jumper Max Rickman. When her mother told her that she'd seen Elena's dad, told him about her and learned that he wanted to meet his daughter, Elena had experienced a host of feelings.

Her first thought was, *Why the hell didn't my mom tell him about me a long time ago? Like when she was pregnant?*

The second thought was the same as the first.

But now she wondered what would happen when she met her dad. *Was she on trial? What if he didn't like her?* If that happened, she didn't think she could stand it.

Now, as she and her mother waited in the Gold Prince Coffeehouse in Ouray for Max to show up, Elena wished again that her mother had told her dad about her in the beginning. Obviously, he cared more than her mom had thought that he would. So who had she been, to make that judgment in the first place? Hadn't he had a *right* to know? And hadn't she, Elena, had a right to know him?

"You're just like Grandma, you know," Elena said.

Jen's eyes snapped toward her. Elena had noticed that her mother was wearing one of her favorite outfits, flowing purple pants and matching top. Her hair was down, too. When she wasn't at work, Jen usually braided it or wore it up, out of the way.

"How am I like Grandma?" Jen demanded.

"He wasn't in love with you, so you kept him from seeing me."

"Excuse me, that is *not* true," Jen exclaimed. She took a sip of her tea.

Jen never drank coffee, Elena knew, because she said it would stain her teeth, which she liked to keep white for the camera.

"It's what you told me," Elena persisted. "You said that he was in love with someone else and so he wouldn't want to know about me. But mostly, you didn't want him to say that he didn't want anything to do with *you*."

Jen sat, stunned not for the first time by her daughter's spontaneous viciousness. "What did I do to deserve this? I saw him. I told him about you."

"Like, twelve *years* after the fact. You still like him," Elena accused. "That's why you're all dressed up."

Jen felt her cheeks flush. "What do you want, Elena? Why are you doing this now?"

Jen saw Max on the sidewalk outside the tall windows. His hair was wind-tousled, and he wore white canvas pants and a white T-shirt with some kind of green design on the front. He opened the door of the coffeehouse, and as he entered he pulled off his aviator sunglasses.

Jen waved, attempting to smile. Was Max, like Elena, going to think she'd "dressed up" for him? She had tried to look her best. She wanted him to find her attractive, yes. But that didn't mean she wanted *him*. Damn Elena. How had she ever learned to be so beastly?

Max's brown eyes strayed to the young girl beside Jen, and Jen saw her daughter stiffen slightly. Elena wore her blond hair up in a French twist. Elena owned three books about braids and up-dos, and together she and Jen had mastered most of the styles. Braces and all, Elena looked older than twelve.

"Hi," Max said, as he reached their table.

"Hi," Elena replied, tight-lipped.

Jen nodded at an empty chair, and Max pulled it out and sat down.

"I'm Max."

"Elena," his daughter answered tersely.

Jen had spoken to Max the previous evening. He'd called her when he'd left the fire crew, and they'd arranged this meeting.

Now, she heard the echoes of Elena's accusations. Max was a *very* attractive man. And he hadn't been in love with her.

And she still wanted to attract him.

"You know, if it's all right," Jen said, "I'd like to leave you two to visit…." There was a bookstore across the street.

"You'll stay here." She gave her daughter a look that meant, *He may be your father, but you better not go anywhere without calling me.* Elena had her cell phone, and Jen had hers. Jen tried to gauge her daughter's reaction to the suggestion.

Elena flatly said, "Sure."

Am I behaving irresponsibly because she was nasty to me? Jen wondered. *Or just to prove that I'm not like my mother?* But surely it wasn't irresponsible to leave her daughter in a public place with Max.

Max said, "You don't *have* to leave."

"You'll be here, right?"

"Not going anywhere," he answered.

"Then I'll see you in a bit." She gave Elena a brief squeeze around the shoulders and walked toward the door, aware of every movement.

Max watched her go. Jen had seemed unusually jumpy—and also keen to get away from this awkward meeting.

How hard could it be to talk to a twelve-year-old girl? His nieces were younger than Elena, and he had no trouble getting along with them.

"Your mom says you're at dance camp."

She nodded, mouth closed. Jen's mouth.

"What kind of dance?" he asked.

"All kinds." Clearly, she didn't want to show her braces. "Afro-Haitian, ballet, jazz, even a little Indian…"

"What's your favorite?"

She seemed to consider. "Ballet, I suppose.

Well, not exactly. It's just that ballet's a good foundation. I love all kinds of African dance. I like modern…cross-cultural."

"I remember your mom was studying dance in school."

"Yeah. She likes African dance, too. She likes everything."

"I brought you something," he said and reached into the breast pocket of his T-shirt. He laid a smoke jumper patch on the table. It bore the insignia of the Alaska smoke jumper crew to which he'd belonged before moving to Leadville, and that morning he'd cut it off the personal-gear bag that went with him on every jump.

"Thanks." She took it, held it, regarded it with an expression of wonder. "I'd like to jump out of an airplane," she said, "but I wouldn't do it."

"Why not?"

"I could get injured. I mean, I want to be a dancer, always, so I won't take risks like that. I don't snowboard, either. I mean, I *can*. I learned when I was little. But one of my friends really messed up her knee skiing."

"It seems as though you might miss out on some fun living by that rule."

She shrugged. "But I love dancing best. I'm not going to do anything that puts my dancing at risk."

Living risks it. He didn't say so, didn't say that things happened in life that were out of a person's control.

"You look like your mom," he said, "but you look kind of like my sister Misty, too."

"You have a sister?"

"Two. One older, one younger. Misty's the younger one. Marina's older."

"You all have names that start with *M*," Elena observed.

"True."

"Was that on purpose?"

"Yes. My mother's choice. You have cousins, too," he told her.

"Do you have pictures?"

"Not with me." He shook his head. "In Leadville."

She blinked. "Leadville?"

"That's where I live in the winter. When it's not fire season."

An expression of either disgust or disillusionment clouded her features.

"What?" he asked.

"How long have you lived in Leadville?"

Now, he identified the expression—
cynicism. "Four years. I'm a forest-service
ranger there. In the winter. There are others
in the summer."

"I can't believe my mom never told you
about me," she said, looking disgusted again.

Over the past few days, he'd had some
trouble believing that himself. Except for the
fact that it was obviously true. Had he been
so cruel to Jen that she'd felt compelled to
protect herself by never saying she was
pregnant? Had she been afraid he'd want her
to have an abortion? In any case, her decision
must have been motivated by his rejection of
her.

It made him angry, and he had no idea if
he had a right to be angry.

He could have been part of this girl's life
from the moment she was born, but Jen had
robbed both him and Elena of the possibility.

How *would* he have reacted if she'd told
him she was pregnant?

He wouldn't have been thrilled.

And he wouldn't have married her.

After Salma died, he'd realized how much
her pregnancy had led to their engagement.
He'd loved her, been enraptured with her.

But he hadn't wanted to be married at twenty-three, let alone be a father at that age.

He would not have done for Jen what he'd been willing to do for Salma. Sure, he would have become involved in Elena's life—he liked to think. But he hadn't been in love with Jennifer Delazzeri.

"She didn't know how I'd react," he finally said.

"Like, so what?"

She had a point.

He changed the subject. "Did your mom tell you what she and I are going to do?"

"No." Wariness crept into her voice, echoing her face.

He reminded himself that Jen hadn't actually agreed. Not yet. "Well, I *hope* she's going to help me. We want to go out to California and investigate the fire we were in together when we were in college."

"Oh, yeah. The one that other girl died in. My aunt was there, too."

"I know. I remember her. We were all good friends."

Elena's expression darkened, then turned haughty. She was mad at someone, but he didn't think it was him. Or maybe it was.

Maybe she was just mad at grown-ups for not being grown-ups.

"My mom hasn't mentioned it. I was pretty surprised she told you about me at all."

Max watched her and listened, hoping she would say more. Finally he asked, "Why?"

"Oh, it's how my family deals with things. Do without Dad. It was how my mom was raised. Her mom thought fathers were expendable."

He'd had no hint of this from Jen. Whether or not it was true, the statement intrigued him. He remembered that Jen's parents had been divorced. He supposed that had shaped his feelings about her. That she was cautious and pragmatic and maybe a bit…remote.

And, as someone whose parents had loved each other and remained together until death intervened, perhaps he had a subtle prejudice against lovers who hadn't had the same experience, perhaps believing that they could never make a permanent union.

He couldn't speak to Elena of his own feelings about Jen's first *not* telling him she was pregnant, then telling him he was the father of a twelve-year-old. And she seemed so much older than a twelve-year-old. He hadn't seen her standing, but he could tell she was tall. And her resemblance to his sister Misty—in the carriage of her head especially—surprised him. It upset him that she was his flesh and blood and yet a stranger to him. It bothered him even more that he was a stranger to her.

How would he tell his family about this?

What would his father say?

That was something Max didn't want to know, didn't want to experience. Because even though Max hadn't known of the pregnancy, his ignorance of the situation somehow would be his fault.

Which was maybe why he lived hundreds of miles from his family. Because whenever he and his father spoke, things became Max's fault that he hadn't known were problems in the first place.

The impossibility of being as good a man as his father, of living up to the standards of Norman Rickman, M.D., hadn't made itself obvious until the Makal Canyon fire. After that…well, now he knew. He and his father had different standards, and if Max tried to live by his father's standards he would never measure up. So his own standards had to be good enough.

Which didn't make it much easier to hear from his father that he wasn't measuring up to *his* standards.

Discovering, at the age of thirty-six, that he had a twelve-year-old daughter was something that would fall far below what Norman Rickman expected of his son.

Revealing that at the age of twenty-three he had made even one woman pregnant— well, the result would have been the same or worse. His father hadn't been keen on Max's engagement to Salma. Max had never told him what had led to it; he never would.

Norman had met Jen, of course, as had Max's sisters. Jen and Teresa and the other hotshots had been to Max's family's house for a party once. And Max's sisters had visited him at the house he'd shared with Salma and the other hotshots, when Jen had lived next door.

But Max doubted that his father had noticed Jen or would remember her.

His instinct surprised him.

He's not going to get to her.

That was the instinct. To protect Jen—and

their daughter, for this young woman was *his* daughter, too—from his father's judgment. Not from a negative judgment, but from the experience of being judged by him.

Norman Rickman did not make mistakes. His life had been one of high achievement and personal sacrifice, and he made sure that everyone knew that was what he was about, which left Max with two thoughts. One, that his father was a great man; and two, that his father was a judgmental man. Which was incompatible with greatness.

"I didn't mean to make you feel bad."

Max blinked. "What? What do you think made me feel bad?"

"What I said," Elena answered, "about fathers being expendable. I didn't mean I think that, or anything."

A generous remark from someone who'd made do without one her whole life.

"I didn't think you meant that. And I don't believe your mother feels that way." *Or she'd never have told me that you exist. Not even after all these years.*

"Well, like, she knew her father, but she never got to see much of him. My grandmother says that he was careless. You know, would drive drunk and stuff."

Driving drunk was, in Max's opinion, more than careless. "It must have frightened her, then," he said, "to think of your mom and your aunt riding around in the car with him."

"Except my mom says he never was drunk when he drove them. She says that my grandmother was jealous of his new wife or his girlfriend or something."

"Do you know him?" Max asked.

"He's dead. I met him when I was a baby, but I don't remember."

"Your mom must be glad that he got to see you."

"I suppose. Anyhow, she's just like my grandmother in her attitudes. I mean, she's not *that* bad." Elena flushed, Max thought, at her own disloyalty.

He said, "In these situations, no one can ever tell how someone else feels. In any situation," he corrected himself.

"Anyhow, why do you want my mom to help you investigate that fire? I mean, she's doing this fire thing for Channel 4, but it's not like she's a scientist or anything."

"That's all right. I want her to help for two reasons. For one, that *is* her area of expertise—being in front of a camera. Interviewing people. The other reason is that she was there. She remembers. She remembers what happened, who else was there, the details."

"What are you going to do when you find out what happened?" Elena asked.

He met her eyes. "I'm not sure. If some people still have jobs they shouldn't have…" he began.

"You want to blame someone," she interrupted.

"I want to make sure that people who made mistakes then don't make the same mistakes again."

"What if no one made mistakes?"

Someone had definitely made mistakes. According to the official investigation report, firefighters, a squad boss. But not a superintendent of hotshots.

Not Richard Grass.

Why do you hate so much after all this time, Max?

Was it injustice that moved him? Was it that Richard had gotten away with near-murder?

He had loved Richard. They all had. Max had trusted Richard's expertise.

Now he thought of Richard as a windbag, someone who'd been happy to dazzle a bunch of kids with his ersatz Oriental wisdom. His aikido and t'ai chi and wing chun kung fu. His pseudo-Tao way of "appreciating" fire.

Then Salma had been killed, and Richard had dodged the responsibility and the accountability.

Like a snake, Max thought.

Yes, he'd like to hang Salma's death on Richard, where it belonged.

"My grandma says that people who set out to get someone back usually end up hurting themselves."

Words of wisdom from the woman who had tried to deprive Jen of a relationship with her father.

"I think anyone who does something wrong would like other people to live by that rule," Max answered. "I mean, they'd like us to forget they did anything wrong and not concern ourselves with seeing justice done."

Elena's eyes narrowed as she studied him.

"What?" he asked.

"Nothing."

"No, you're thinking something."

"Well—I don't go to Sunday school or anything. That's not the kind of family we have. We're sort of more into, I don't know, the power of women than Jesus."

He listened, and didn't bother to tell her that his impression was that Jesus had liked women just fine. He wasn't religious and he didn't care enough about the subject to argue with anyone.

"But don't a lot of religions," she asked, "say that people aren't supposed to concern themselves with dishing out judgment?"

"Look at it this way," he told her. "Say your mom, or... No, say someone else you care about gets murdered. Wouldn't you want to see that person's murderer go to jail?"

"It wouldn't bring the person back to life."

"But say that putting the person in jail kept him from killing anyone else."

"I can see that," she said. "But nobody got murdered in the fire, did they? Wasn't it just an accident?"

"When you're supposed to be doing a job and you make a mistake and people get hurt—" thinking of Jackson, he winced slightly "—it's never just an accident." He watched her face. Here he'd known his daughter half an hour, at most, and he was trying to influence her thinking on moral issues. What if he taught her the wrong thing?

Had his parents ever wondered if what they taught him was wrong?

His father hadn't, that was for certain. Norman Rickman knew what was right and suffered no other opinions.

Being a physician, for example, was right.

For a person intelligent enough to become a physician, becoming something less—a smoke jumper, for instance—was wrong, a squandering of divine gifts.

But I like fighting fires, Max had told him.

It's doubtful if a lot of those fires should even be fought, his father had replied.

Sometimes we let them burn.

Well, thank God for moments of sanity.

And so on.

Max seldom thought of these exchanges any more. But finding out that he himself was a father changed that. Now he examined one bygone argument with his father after another.

"Where did you grow up?" Elena asked.

"A place called Carpinteria in California. My father still lives there." He wouldn't have attended graduate school so close to home except that the University of California at Santa Barbara had offered the program he'd wanted. And back then he'd valued his father and his sisters especially highly. His mother hadn't been dead all that long. Family mattered.

They still mattered.

And if he returned to Makal Canyon with Jen, he couldn't escape seeing them. Because Makal Canyon was in the mountains above Carpinteria.

In any event, whether in person or by long distance, he would have to tell his father that he was a grandfather once again.

He would have to tell his father how, and how it happened that he hadn't known.

Max dreaded it—for himself, for Jen and for Elena.

"Would you like to come out to California with us?" he asked Elena. "And meet your cousins?"

"I guess."

He'd heard more enthusiasm from smoke

jumpers preparing for a long pack out after a fire.

He eyed her curiously.

"What's out there? Am I going to be hiking around with you and my mom, trying to find out about the fire?"

"We'll probably manage to have some fun, too. Have you ever been to the ocean?"

"Yes." A touch of resentment in the answer. *Did you think I had no life before you decided to be part of it?*

"I could teach you to surf."

"I might get injured," she pointed out. "It wouldn't be worth it."

"You've never surfed. So how would you know?"

"I love to dance. That's all I need to know."

Someone, he thought, had done a good job on her. No risk, no risking her future, which she was so certain would involve dancing professionally.

You're twelve years old! he wanted to say. *Live a little.*

But what right did he have to say anything of the kind, to try to shape who she was at all?

His jaw tightened.

He *hadn't* wanted this. But now he was in. And he had as much right to take part in Elena Delazzeri's life as he would have if her mother had told him she was pregnant thirteen years before.

He was going to exercise that right—though not in order to live up to the standards of Norman Rickman.

But simply because now he had met his daughter.

And now, he didn't *want* to walk away, and he knew he never would.

"I HAVEN'T EVEN SAID I'll take part in that project!" Jen exclaimed angrily, when Elena told her what she and Max had discussed. "How dare he invite you along, when he doesn't even know if I'm going to take part?"

Jen was tired and edgy. Still in some pain from her burns, bored from wandering in and out of shops while Max and Elena had their first conversation, annoyed at having been accused by her daughter of first one thing and then another. Now, this.

"You just don't want me to be around him," Elena said.

"Nonsense. I arranged this meeting, didn't I?"

"But you didn't think I'd like him, did you?"

How unfair. "I thought you probably would like him."

"But you thought I'd just want our life to go on the way it has been, as if I hadn't met him."

"Elena, why are you doing this?" Jen demanded through gritted teeth as she drove her Subaru station wagon back to Denver. "You're making all kinds of suppositions on a subject you know almost nothing about. You wanted to meet your father and I was able to make it happen."

"You could have made it happen *before* I was born, instead of waiting till I was twelve. What were you afraid of? He wasn't going to hold anything against me. Just against you."

"I don't deserve this."

"I want to go to Makal Canyon," said Elena. "And I want to go to Carpinteria and meet my cousins. I have a whole bunch of relatives you never even would have told me about."

"Elena, the meeting today did not happen by accident. And since Max is not psychic, it *wouldn't* have happened if I hadn't taken steps to bring the two of you together."

"You just hate men," Elena said. "Like Grandma and Teresa."

"I do not hate men. In fact, I like them." Jen tried to think of what she'd done to explain her daughter's constant attacks for the past twenty-four hours or so. "I'm sorry," she said, "that you have not had the benefit of knowing your father your whole life. I'm glad you've met him now."

" 'Have met him now'?" said Elena. "You say that like that's the end of it, like I'm never going to see him again."

"He works long hours. It may not be convenient for—"

"You don't want me to have a relationship with him, do you? Because he doesn't want to be with *you*. Just like Grandma. You're exactly the same."

"I am not the same as your grandmother."

"Could have fooled me."

Jen wondered if a more irritating twelve-year-old had ever walked the earth. "For twelve years," she said tightly, "I have supported you, done my very best by you, given you almost everything you've wanted. I've driven you to dance classes, enrolled you in workshops and camp…"

"So that buys you off? I thought my father must be, like, sleazy or something," Elena said, "since you didn't want me to meet him. I thought there was something wrong with him."

"But I told you the truth."

"I didn't think anything that lame could possibly be true!"

Jen heard the last words she herself had spoken. *The truth.*

Had she really told Elena the truth?

Not the whole truth, because the whole truth included Max and Jen making love just hours after his fiancée had *died* of burns. Jen understood very well that death often had that effect on people. But Elena was not an adult and shouldn't be expected to understand that.

Just how did Max plan to pull off the Makal Canyon documentary with Elena on the scene—without Elena learning that Max had been engaged to the only person who'd died in the fire?

Of course, Jen had already revealed that he'd loved Salma.

But being engaged was different, and it would be seen differently by a twelve-year-old.

Furthermore, there was no making Elena see that it wasn't that unnatural for her mother and Max to have made love not long after his fiancée's death.

Jen could hardly wait until she had a chance to talk privately with Max and point these things out to him. In any event, she'd had just about enough sass from her daughter.

"Let's get something straight, all right?"

"Yes," snapped Elena. They were driving into Grand Junction, and Elena was already searching the radio for music, emphasizing that nothing her mother had to say was of importance.

Jen punched off the radio. "Whatever you think, I am not carrying a torch for someone I haven't seen for thirteen years. None of my decisions concerning you—" *lately,* she silently added "—have come about because I still like your father or want him to like me. When you're twelve, maybe it seems possible that something like that can happen.

"But it doesn't happen, all right? I got over him so long ago that I was a completely different person then. People don't keep on being attracted to the same people they liked in college."

"That's not true! People get married in college and stay together!"

She was right, of course. "Fine. But that's not the case here. I got over him and made my own life."

Elena said, "What *you* have is a life?"

Jen snapped the radio back on.

"Fine," her daughter added, as if she hadn't already had the last word. "Don't talk about it."

"Fine," Jen answered. "I won't."

CHAPTER SIX

CHANNEL 4 CAMERAMAN Bob Wright had been an audio-visual geek in high school and had then gone on to earn a master's of fine arts in audio-visual geekdom. This is what he'd told Jen when he'd met her. He had the kind of light hair she thought of as "fish" blond, freckles and blue eyes.

When she told him she'd handed in her resignation at Channel 4, he simply said, "Me, too. So you're going to Makal Canyon with us, then?"

She had not agreed to go to Makal Canyon and was actually considering a job offer from an Albuquerque station. Elena had greeted this news with the observation that her mother was "only doing this so I'll be farther from my dad. It's like a demotion, Mom."

Not a demotion. A change. A smart change.

"No," she told Bob. "I don't think I am."

"Well, I am."

"This is a good job for you," she said. "Why are you walking away from it?"

He didn't answer, and she knew why no answer came. He blamed himself for the burns that John Jackson had sustained. He felt he'd been too protective of the camera.

He now made daily excursions to the burn center at the Denver hospital to which the smoke jumper had been transferred. He and Jackson had become friends, in a way. Max had been to see him, too.

In three cell phone conversations with Max since his meeting with Elena in Ouray, Jen had refused to commit to the documentary. Her objection that she couldn't afford to stay away from work that long was flimsy, and she knew it. She had some money from her father's death, set aside for a time when she needed it. And her mother had enough money to buy Jen out of Jen's share in the house where they lived—except that the house had appreciated so much since they'd bought it. Anyway, the whole thing was complicated. But Max had also offered her money for working on the film.

No, she just couldn't get excited about going back to Makal Canyon with Max Rickman, with or without Elena. Jen kept praying that overtime—smoke jumper's paradise—would keep Max too busy to see his daughter again.

It hadn't kept him too busy to call Elena, however, and now, according to her, they talked every day that he wasn't on a fire.

Jen's mother had already begun to deliver dark hints and warnings. *He could be a gold digger for all you know. Don't forfeit any of your parental rights. He should be made to pay child support.*

The phrase that rang in Jen's ears, an echo of what she still believed lay behind her mother's years of determination to keep Jen's father from seeing Jen and Teresa was, "He should be made to pay…"

What bothered Jen most was that sentiments very like that sometimes suggested themselves to her in regard to Max Rickman.

Jen couldn't help but notice that Max's appearance in their lives seemed to have been a catalyst, turning her daughter into a tyrant. Now, every evening Jen was subjected to some form or another of condemnation from her daughter. Jen couldn't see what Elena hoped to attain. *Inflicting guilt?* Her nastiness actually chipped away the guilt that Jen felt.

Embarrassment? Yes, in retrospect, she was embarrassed that she had not told Max she was pregnant—or told him when their child was born.

And every evening, Elena wanted to know if they would be going to California with Max.

Jen had asked Elena not to mention Makal Canyon in front of Teresa, saying that it could send her aunt into a downward spiral.

So instead Elena brought it up every time she and Jen were alone.

WHEN HE BROUGHT UP Makal Canyon, Bob said, "Jen, it would be fun to work together."

As it always had been. They'd become good friends working together covering the Rocky Mountains news.

As the two of them waited for the elevator to take them down to the station's parking garage, Jen told him, "I always like working with you, but trust me, Max's film is a project with no meaningful future."

"It's for fire education," Bob said. "After what happened out at Silver Jack, I think there can't be too much of that."

Yes, and I've been on a fire where someone died, someone I knew, a housemate, my sister's best friend, almost like another sister to me... And Max's fiancée, carrying his child.

"Please think about it Jen. He'll want to interview you even if you're not part of the project, because you were at the fire."

Bob and Max had clearly done some talking about the film. Why was Bob getting sucked into Max's stupid quest for revenge?

Jen studied Bob's face. He was shaky again today. The fire had changed him. Maybe he needed to help on the Makal Canyon project as some sort of penance.

"I'll think about it," she told him as the elevator doors slid open.

"I SUGGESTED a different location for Helispot Two," Max repeated to the fire investigator, whom he was getting to know better than he had wanted to. Together they'd spent hours looking at aerial photographs, Max's photos and those taken by others at the fire, topographical maps and the log of the Silver Jack fire. Max and the superintendent had been interviewed together and separately about the fateful selection of the helspot. Max, Tock, the helicopter pilot and others had been questioned about the arrival of the news crew of two. But even now Max felt as if he was deflecting responsibility for the choice of the second helicopter base to the hotshot supervisor, rather than accepting his own part of it.

Of course, he'd said that he had, in the end, agreed. He'd said that he now heartily wished he'd insisted on a different location.

But a helicopter had brought the hotshots to Silver Jack, to the ridge. The smoke jumpers had arrived by jump plane. Max told himself that the hotshot superintendent's stake in the choice had been greater; that's why he, Max, had yielded.

But is your part, Max, so different from what Richard Grass's was thirteen years ago?

Yes.

"And did you see John Jackson take the television camera from—" the investigator consulted his notes "—Bob Wright?"

"Yes." Though he hadn't seen Jackson take the camera with him into his shelter, hadn't understood Jackson's intention to shelter up *with* the camera. It went against the grain to argue these facts now. Because if he'd seen it, what would he have done? Would he have insisted that Jackson leave the expensive piece of equipment outside his shelter?

Max knew only that he himself wouldn't have taken responsibility for the camera. The camera had belonged to Channel 4. His mandate had been to protect *people* at the helicopter base and to put out fire, not care for equipment belonging to civilians or to a television station.

He'd assumed, he supposed, that Jackson would set down the camera somewhere it would be at least partially protected from flames, not within his fire shelter. But this was speculation on Max's part; he actually couldn't remember what had gone through his mind when he'd seen Jackson take the camera, beyond relief that one of the smoke jumpers had taken it. The camera was out of Bob Wright's hands; Bob Wright was being made as safe as was possible. He, Max, would make sure that Jen opened her fire shelter, deployed it properly. He would look after both individuals. Those had been his thoughts. Once the camera was gone from Bob's hands, Max hadn't given it another thought.

I didn't believe Jackson would take it in his shelter with him.

But was he remembering this correctly? The temptation to remember things in a way that made him look or feel better was tempting yet unspoken.

"Now, I've learned something interesting. That you and Jennifer Delazzeri knew each other before this fire. That in fact you'd shared a shelter during a previous fire, in—" another glance at his notes "—Makal Canyon."

"Yes. We were Santa Inez Hotshots together. She was a rookie, and my understanding is that she left fire fighting after that fire." *My understanding.* He knew damn well she hadn't fought another fire. That he and Jen had ever shared the intimacy of lovers was none of the fire investigator's business.

"Do you think you might have been distracted by her presence?"

"She's an attractive woman. We were all

distracted. I don't think it interfered with my attention to my job, though."

"Yes, but you *knew* her. You greeted each other as old friends."

Max said nothing.

"Do you think John Jackson might have been sufficiently distracted by the presence of Ms. Delazzeri to forget his training?"

"I don't think he *forgot* his training at all. I think he disregarded it, and I'm sure he's told you the same thing."

The investigator neither confirmed nor denied this supposition. He had come to Leadville to meet with Max in the forest service offices. *Following up,* he said.

The questions to which Max most wanted answers—whether or not mistakes made at Silver Jack would affect his career path in firefighting—couldn't be answered. Nonetheless, he'd already arranged for time off in August to go to Makal Canyon. Bob Wright had agreed to come; Elena wanted to come. Jen didn't want Elena accompanying him, and she didn't want to go herself.

Max had tried to persuade her to have dinner with him to talk it over, and her response still made him smile.

Oh, that would go over well at this end. Elena thinks I didn't tell you about her earlier because I've carried a torch for you all these years.

She'd sounded indignant.

He'd said, *Well, I don't think either of us was going to forget the other.*

No answer to that.

He would call her again when the investigator was through with him.

"NOTHING IS DIFFERENT from the last time you asked me," she snapped impatiently.

"Are you at work?" he asked.

"No, I'm on my way to a class."

"Dance?"

"No."

"Should I call when you're not driving?"

"I'm not driving. I'm walking at the moment. What do you want? Same old, same old?"

"Yes. I want you and Elena to come back to Makal Canyon."

He heard her sigh. "Since I've introduced you and Elena, I've traded a reasonably lev-elheaded child for a moody adolescent who blames me for everything that's gone wrong her whole life. And if that weren't enough to convince me that going to California is a bad idea, there's her likely reaction to the thought of you and me in bed together seconds after your fiancée died."

"People react that way to death all the time." Wondering if it would behoove him to act as if their frantic couplings had been more than that, he said, "Not that it was that simple."

"Wasn't it?" She sounded bored, distant.

"Look, if she hadn't been injured, it wouldn't have happened. Not then anyhow." Not ever, because he would have married Salma and been the father of *her* child instead of the father of Elena.

He didn't wish that had been the case—not exactly. Elena was there, and she was his daughter, and now that he'd met her there was no going back.

"Don't you think Elena's likely to find out eventually that Salma and I were engaged?"

"How?" Jen demanded. "Are you planning to tell her? She'll turn on you next."

Clearly, Jen resented her daughter's wavering allegiance.

"I'll tell her to be more respectful to you."

"She's spent her whole life, *until* now, being respectful to me!" Jen exclaimed, and then fell silent.

"Really?" he asked.

A slight pause. "Most of the time." As she hurried down the sidewalk toward the Lodo martial arts center where she practiced, studied and taught fighting arts, she wondered, not for the first time, at Max's motivation for involving her in the Makal Canyon project. She wondered about the real reasons behind his wanting to do the project at all. Could asking *again* hurt? "Max, why are you doing this? Really? The documentary."

"To help future firefighters not make—or agree to—the mistakes that were made that day."

"I don't believe you."

"Why not?"

"Because you've always struck me as being realistic. And to me it seems unrealistic to think that anyone is really going to pay attention to the lessons of that fire. What fire lessons haven't been taught before?"

"First of all, no one pays attention to where that subdivision was built. Nobody really talks about that, about assessing a building site for wildfire *before* the threat materializes."

"The fire never touched the subdivision," Jen said, knowing that wasn't the point and knowing that her saying so would simply annoy him. Annoying him didn't bother her; she herself was annoyed. Possibly annoyed that she, a thirty-two-year-old professional woman, a television newscaster, should still in some way not be good enough for Max Rickman.

That was a judgment, of course—she had no way of knowing if she wasn't "good enough" for him. In his eyes, that is. In her own eyes, at least, she ought to be good enough.

Ought to. There was the rub. *He rejected you, and while your heart has recovered, your pride will never forget.*

So maybe her daughter's accusations weren't that far off the mark.

"Suppose," she said, "that I say I'll do it. I have to ask you again what you think Elena's reaction will be to finding out that we were lovers so soon after your fiancée's death."

"I think she'll surprise you."

"How?"

"By showing you more maturity than you expect. Either that, or she simply won't care."

Did Jen want her to care?

"I'm sure," Max added, "that she is going to do as little thinking about you and me together in bed as possible, because she probably finds the whole idea revolting."

"You'd pay me?" she finally said. "Some kind of stipend?"

"Ten grand, plus expenses."

That was a lot of money for a month's work, if that was all the time the film turned out to take, which seemed doubtful.

"All right. I'll do it." If only to prove to Max, to Elena, and most of all to herself, that her pride had recovered from the blow Max Rickman had dealt it—and her— thirteen years before.

TERESA'S VOICE DID NOT SOUND quite normal to Jen. Her sister greeted her when she arrived home from class. As Jen dropped her tote bag in her room in the two-storey brick house the family shared, Teresa stood in the doorway fidgeting.

People never thought that she and Teresa were sisters. While Jen was dark-haired and brown-eyed, Teresa was blond and blue-eyed, like their mother. In college, her hair had been a mop of loose curls, her smile disarming. Since then, however, she'd gained weight and cut her hair very short.

And of course, there were the side effects of her meds.

Jen reminded herself that mental illness ran in families and that it existed in hers. It was too easy to want to shout, *Look what that stupid fire did to my sister!*

Max would argue that he was simply trying to determine who was to blame for the disaster.

Jen wanted to forget the damned fire.

Of course, she never would. And Teresa definitely never would.

"Max called."

Jen tensed, hearing these words spoken in Teresa's slurred speech.

"I guess," Teresa continued, her voice showing more strain, rising in pitch, "he's pretty glad to know Elena now. That must make you happy."

"Yes," Jen said. Then she added, "He *ought* to be glad. He's *lucky* to know her."

"He says…" again that strained, unnatural note "…you're going back to Makal Canyon to work on a documentary together. He invited me to come."

Jen swore silently. Max had invited Teresa, and it was already having a negative effect on her sister.

"I said I can't afford it," Teresa said, "and he offered to pay my way and put me up there. Do you think it would be wrong for me to accept?"

Her sister was so scrupulous. While Jen focused on not turning into her mother, Teresa fretted over etiquette.

"No," Jen said flatly. "He wants your help with the film, and he should damn well pay for it."

"He said he might find work for me."

Jen wished that Max Rickman was within the reach of her hands right now.

"You and Elena and I could all room together," Teresa continued. "That wouldn't mean accepting so much from him."

"Teresa Delazzeri, I have single-handedly raised his child for the past twelve years. I'm telling you, take anything he offers."

"You sound like Mom."

"I do not!"

"That's just what she used to tell us to do with Dad. She always said he didn't pay enough child support."

"He didn't," interjected a new voice.

Their mother had joined them. Robin Delazzeri was still a beautiful woman. She wore her white hair in a braid and dressed in elegant, flowing clothing. After retiring from nursing, she'd begun volunteering at a physical therapy center. She kept in shape with weights, yoga, daily walks, hiking in the summer and downhill skiing in the winter.

Robin turned to her younger daughter. "Teresa says that she talked to Max and you're all going out to California. You and Elena and Max, that is, and Teresa if she wants to go."

"Will you be all right?" Jen asked.

"Why don't I come with you?"

Because you're not invited. But Jen didn't say that, she just knew an inner exasperation—and a feeling of sympathy for her father.

"I don't have to *stay* with you. I could see friends in Monterey."

"Why would you want to come?" Jen asked.

"Because I'm your mother. I like to keep my nest together."

I've left the damned nest. We live in the same house, and I pay half the mortgage. Jen wished that her mother would find someone to date. Whenever she did, it distracted her from trying to control the other people in her life. Boundaries, boundaries, boundaries. The last time her mother had violated them left and right was when Teresa had briefly dated someone. Before that, it was Jen's most recent lover.

She sounds narcissistic, a therapist had told Jen. *And histrionic.*

So this trip, if she decided to go, would involve another power struggle with Robin. The prospect exhausted Jen.

Should Teresa come to California? Leaving her sister behind would take up some of her mother's energy, at least. Anyhow, what would it do to Teresa, revisiting the scene of the fire that had changed her life and ended the life of her best friend?

It's not my decision, Jen told herself. *Teresa's an adult.*

"Well," said Robin, in a petulant voice that Jen knew well, "I'm off to yoga. Elena's in her room. She has some news for you, I think."

What news could Elena have that she hadn't rushed out to share with her mother? Jen wondered.

She headed down the hallway and knocked on the door of her daughter's room.

"Come in, Mom."

Jen opened the door. Elena's room was white and decorated with modern furniture. Instead of posters of rock stars—or even famous ballerinas—on her walls, she'd hung some small, minimalist art pieces, most of which she'd talked Robin into buying for her.

Elena stood in the middle of her room in a pair of black jazz pants and crop top, still dressed from her dance class that afternoon. "Guess what?"

Jen lifted her eyebrows, waiting.

"Michelle is choreographing a performance piece for the arts council banquet, and she has asked me to do a solo, to promote the school and the company."

"Wow. That's great. Where is it going to be?"

The details flowed forth and in the midst of

her recitation Elena reached for her cell phone. "I forgot to tell Max. I want him to come."

Elena hadn't yet begun calling him Dad. Jen wondered if she ever would. "What's the date?"

"September fourth. It's ringing." She began jumping up and down.

"But if we go to Makal Canyon with Max, you won't be able to do it. You won't be here for rehearsals."

Elena heard. Gaped, half listening to a recorded message on the phone. "It's Elena. Call me. I have something to tell you." She snapped shut her phone. "We're *going? You're* going?"

"Don't you want me to?" A fear came to Jen—that Elena would prefer to spend the time alone with Max. Of course, it was natural that she'd want to spend some time alone with him. He'd already mentioned the possibility of a father-daughter backpacking trip in the Maroon Bells-Snowmass Wilderness or in one of Colorado's other federal wilderness areas.

If that happened, Jen would be amazed. Elena did not like camping. She was a city girl and happy to stay that way.

Their cat walked into the room. She was

butterscotch-and-white, long-haired, with fur that seemed to stick out at strange angles, giving her a rakish look. During much of her childhood, Elena had begged for a variety of pets, nearly all of them impractical. For instance, she'd wanted a dog—but not just any dog. She'd wanted a Rhodesian Ridgeback that she could show in the ring—a hobby about which Jen knew practically nothing—and breed.

Then, it was one of those potbellied pigs.

An Arctic fox.

A miniature horse.

Then, a variety of exotic cats. Jen had briefly considered that, until she'd realized that those which her daughter wanted had to be kept in steel cages and shouldn't be handled by anyone who wasn't wearing leather gloves and a face guard.

For a time, Elena had actually owned a Bearded Dragon, but it had died earlier in this season of fire—from smoke in the air.

Now, Elena turned away and went to sit at her desk. "So, if we go to California—when are you going to do it?"

"August, as I understand it. Maybe the end of July."

"Could I stay here part of the time, and fly out to be with you guys when I don't have to rehearse? Then Grandma wouldn't be so lonely, anyway."

And Robin would stay in Denver.

Nonetheless, Jen couldn't afford the plane tickets, not since she'd just quit her job. One round trip ticket, yes. More—no.

"We'll talk about it."

"But you're definitely going?" Elena's eyes veiled her emotions, whatever they were.

"Yes," Jen said. "Definitely."

CHAPTER SEVEN

MAX KNEW he should prepare his father for the reality of Elena, but by the end of July he still hadn't told anyone in his family that he had a daughter. On the twenty-fifth, he picked up Bob Wright, Jen and Teresa and headed for the airport. Elena would fly out later, for three four-day visits at his expense.

Max sat beside Jen on the flight to Santa Barbara. The computer animation tech for their project would pick them up and drive them to the house they would share in Canyon Wind Estates—the subdivision that had been saved from the fire in which Salma had been fatally burned.

Max insisted that Jen take the window seat, and as she gazed out the window he watched the curve of her jaw beneath the hair she'd braided into an elegant and artful twist high on her head. Today, she wore purple again, some pants that clung to her body, emphasizing the muscles she obviously took care to maintain, and a purple camisole, with a blue hooded cardigan.

She seemed so remote—more than she had on Silver Jack Ridge, before he'd known about Elena. Yet now her inner self was hidden, perhaps so that he couldn't reject it again.

That rejection haunted him. He couldn't forget the things she claimed he'd said. Things that sounded like something he could have said. That their sexual experience was only about sex. That it had happened because of the fire. That he did not love her.

He couldn't imagine saying the last to a woman now. He had slept with women he didn't quite love, but he certainly didn't announce the fact that he didn't. Why had he needed to say such a thing to Jen?

Because what they'd done was too much like love—and Salma had only just died.

Teresa had begged for a solo seat, in the back, and Bob had taken the other. Halfway into the flight, Max stood up to see how they were doing. Bob was talking animatedly to a businessman across the aisle. Teresa was reading a book by Ayn Rand and seemed not to be looking at anyone.

Jen asked, "What's she doing?"

"Reading." He took his seat again.

The plane was too full for Jen to wander back and engage her sister in conversation. But it bothered her that Teresa had wanted to sit alone.

What Teresa had said, however, was, *No, you two sit together.*

Well, maybe that's what it was all about—wanting Jen to be friends with Max.

Jen didn't feel much like his friend. Old hurts and recent indignation seemed to overshadow other feelings. And why couldn't she come to terms with that long-ago rejection?

Men found her attractive. Some recognized her from the news, yes, and others simply found her to be a pretty woman. She was asked on dates, asked to join men skiing, horseback riding. But she accepted few invitations, and now Elena had accused her of hating men.

She didn't hate them. She was wary of them. First of all, it was damned hard to find a good man, a man she *wanted* to date. But even if she found one, as far as she was concerned falling in love was as welcome as being bitten by something poisonous. It just seemed to come with pain. Even men she liked—but with whom she wasn't in love—could cause hurt, though not on the scale she might experience if she fell in love.

As she once had with Max.

Four weeks. Four weeks they would all live together in a house at Canyon Winds Estates. She'd told him that was it. She had to be back with her daughter for the start of school. Though she wasn't sure she'd be returning to Denver in the fall. Jen had always been attracted to the educational opportunities in Albuquerque, both for herself and Elena.

She'd resigned from Channel 4, and she'd told the Albuquerque station that she would give them a decision by the third week in August.

What will Mom and Teresa do without you?

Manage.

The truth was, she wasn't sure she wanted to stay in television. She'd have to get out sometime; maybe now was the time, when she was beginning to yearn for something different. Just what, she wasn't sure. But for years she'd been fascinated by acupuncture and Oriental medicine. Or perhaps she might look into in-depth training as a massage therapist? Or a counseling degree? Something like Oriental medicine or even massage therapy would blend well with her interest in martial arts. What she was beginning to feel was the need to move on. She was compassionate and she was good at her job. But John Jackson's being burned while protecting that damned camera had soured the whole business for her. They shouldn't have been up there at all, and she'd known it.

"What are you thinking?" Max asked.

"Just—dreaming. About getting out of television."

"I'm surprised you didn't become a dancer."

"I'll always be a dancer." Though now her form of dance involved the fighting arts— evasion, grace, flexibility.

"I just pictured you traveling the world, free-spirited, maybe a choreographer."

She smiled slightly. "I'm sure you didn't picture me nine months pregnant or with a new baby." Again, she wished she could take back her words. Why did she need to rub his face in what he hadn't known? She could have told him she was pregnant, after all.

Max slid his day pack partially out from under his seat and withdrew a textbook. Something on fire behavior.

"You love fire, don't you?" she asked.

"I love fighting fires, watching them as a natural phenomenon. Sure. I don't have to be out there, though."

"So you could move up to being a fire general, so to speak. Strategizing how to put out the big fires."

"That's the plan."

"Don't you think you might be rubbing the right people the wrong way by making this film?"

"Actually, no. Not if it can be used as an educational tool for firefighters."

Jen fell silent.

He said, "So tell me. Any men in your life?"

"No. I think you've asked me that."

"Have you ever, say, lived with someone?"

Now you're trying to make me out to be some kind of romantic failure, Jen thought,

just because I've never lived with a man.
"That's not a decision I'd ever have made
casually—around Elena. You know. Bringing a man into her life that way."

His eyebrows lifted slightly.

"Well, it's not," Jen snapped. "It takes a
long time to get to know someone and trust
him."

"You trusted me fast enough."

"You used to be my next-door neighbor, my
squad boss. We were hotshots together, and
I've known you a long time, even though we
haven't been in touch. And you're mistaken,
anyway, if you think I trust you. But you're her
natural father. She needs to know you."

Jen's prickly edges surprised Max, surprised him again and again. She'd changed
from when they'd lived together, yes. But it
seemed as though more than simple maturity
had shaped her. Her life, her all-female household, her job, everything about her, now
seemed carefully designed to protect Jen Delazzeri. But from what? What did she think
would happen to her if she relaxed just a little?

He picked over the various ways of putting
the question to her, rejecting each one in turn.
He'd noticed what happened whenever he

became curious about her personal life. When he tried, she responded with reminders of the sacrifices she'd made to raise his daughter.

"You must get along with your mom pretty well," he said.

"Sometimes. Most of the time, in fact, now that I'm an adult."

"It seems unusual, to me, for a grown woman to be able to live with her mother."

"She has always helped me with Elena." Now Jen sounded defensive again.

"I wasn't criticizing you," he told her.

"But I feel like you're picking me apart!"

He studied her aquiline nose, her smooth olive-toned skin and her freckles. "I'm just trying to know you, Jen. And to know my daughter by finding out what I can about how she has grown up."

"She has grown up without a father." Jen heard herself with disgust. *Why* did she keep doing this? It was as if she couldn't control herself.

"You resent that," Max said.

Jen shook her head. "I don't know what's wrong with me. I'm sorry I said that. I'm responsible for not telling you about her."

What would it cost her to say the honest thing? She eyed the people across the aisle. Was anyone eavesdropping, listening to this conversation in which she was so vulnerable. No and no one could really overhear them. She and Max were talking quietly. "Okay," she said. "The truth is, I felt much more for you than you did for me, and I was hurt by it, and whenever I remember that I start saying all these…things." *I start turning into my mother.* Wasn't that what had been behind her mother's drama? Jen's father had not been a bad person. His only crime had been to fall out of love with Robin.

But Jen could never speak of that to anyone outside the family. In fact, even she and Teresa didn't discuss it much anymore. Teresa suffered from one form of instability; Jen thought their mother had some other variety, maybe a personality disorder. Jen had always sworn that Elena's upbringing would not be like her own.

Yet I denied her a relationship with her father for twelve years.

She didn't know how she expected Max to respond to her confession that she'd been hurt. By saying he was sorry?

But of their individual sins, hers had been the greater. He'd been a college student whose fiancée had just died. Jen couldn't believe that he'd set out intending to use her.

Yet she had kept from him the knowledge that she was carrying his child. Now, in her mind, the action mimicked the spirit of every effort her own mother had made to keep Jen and Teresa from seeing their father.

Max said, "Tell me how you got into martial arts."

"How did you—"

"Elena. What styles do you practice?"

"Well, my focus is Muay Thai, Thai boxing."

"Is that the same as kickboxing?"

"Close. A little more hard-core. I've learned some aikido, as well, and played *capoeira,* which is a Brazilian combat game, very challenging—and fun for a dancer. And now I'm learning fundamentals from some Indonesian fighting arts. But mostly I'm a Thai boxer."

"Can't you hurt your head?"

"You bet."

"You shouldn't do that."

"Well, in sparring situations we learn to

exercise a lot of control, to protect ourselves and each other. We don't go to class and try to knock each other out."

A small smile spread on his face.

"What?"

"I'm a little envious. I'd like to learn a martial art. Sometimes. Truthfully, Richard tainted the whole thing for me, doing what he did."

"Which was…" It was time, Jen decided, to hear exactly what part Max believed Richard Grass had played in Salma's death.

He didn't answer at once. He glanced toward the window, then at his watch, then withdrew a legal pad from his pack and began to sketch, taking her back to the day of the Makal Canyon blowup.

She remembered that day, even as she didn't want to remember. The fire had crept below them from the west, reaching the two of them first. The other group had been cutting fire line by the road, against the estates, which had been built in the worst possible location from a wildfire standpoint. "We couldn't reach them by radio because of the terrain. That big gully." Her heart began beating faster, a little too fast for a person who wasn't presently in danger. She shouldn't have agreed to do this. She didn't *want* to remember. She'd been at the Silver Jack fire, in a second burnover, where she'd heard someone being burned. Yet it was the Makal Canyon fire that resurrected all her ghosts, for they were ghosts of that blaze.

I'm not sure I'm going to be able to do this.

But this was the kind of thought she never let herself feel, let alone voice. Because of her mother, of course. Robin had feigned weakness—or been weak, at times, because her jealousy had led her to lie. And so Jen must never appear weak; must never be weak.

Her mother was foremost in her mind these days, ever since Max had come back into her life—and entered Elena's life. Now her daughter had a father, and Jen felt herself in danger of becoming like her own mother.

Max said, "Cast your mind back, Jen. Were we in more live fuels or dead fuels?"

"My ability to answer that question could be based on recollection—or on my study of the investigation report." Which she had reviewed over the two previous days. It had placed blame on the hotshots for working on southwest-facing slopes, where the fire had gotten below them. It hadn't mattered, the report implied, who'd told them to work there. Hadn't they been trained?

That had angered her. Still, why was Max so bent on doing this documentary? *I just want to forget it. Forgive and especially forget.*

Her mother had total recall for every one of the actual sins of Jen's father, plus all those she'd manufactured. It had been sad to watch. Robin was so beautiful, and all her efforts to get back together with Gino Delazzeri had driven him further away. Her invitations to him to take in a movie with them had never seemed to bother him, but her insistence on controlling him and his contact with Jen and Teresa, most of all the way Robin had used Jen and Teresa in their ongoing conflict, had enraged him. Sometimes, Jen had wondered if her mother was *trying* to drive their father to violence, so that she could call the police— which she did anyway—and say, *I told you so.*

Finally, Jen answered Max's question. "It was the third year of drought. There were plenty of dead fuels." The plane had begun its descent, and she looked out the window.

Flying into Santa Barbara brought back so much. "I haven't been to California since I moved away."

"Which was when?"

"Elena was five. I got the job offer with Channel 4, and my mother had the opportunity to study yoga with a teacher she'd admired for years. So we moved to Denver, bought our house, and that was that."

"Where were you until then?"

"Well, Mom still had the house in Monterey, but she was down with Teresa and me a lot because of Elena. And Teresa."

"Because all of you needed her after the fire."

He said this as if Elena had been part of the fire. Jen said, "The fire is not part of Elena's life and never has been. You and Teresa and I were at the fire, but Elena was conceived afterward. You know that. Everything in the world is not about your fiancée dying in that stupid fire."

It had happened again. She'd said things she'd never intended to say, things she wasn't aware of thinking before she spoke.

"Is that why you think I'm doing this?" he asked. "You think I'm not over that?"

"Do people get over it?" Jen asked. "I'm not sure they do. I don't think Teresa has."

"But she was with Salma. She witnessed more than we did."

"We all *saw* her, Max. Everyone saw the shape she was in. Everyone knew how bad it was and that she might not make it. I don't think *I'm* over it, if it comes to that. I didn't volunteer to cover the Silver Jack fire, you know. I was sent."

Max experienced a strange shock again, a sort of electricity. Her honesty was something alive; something that made him more alive.

I always liked her.

Yes, Salma had been his girlfriend, his lover, his fiancée, but he'd always noticed Jen Delazzeri, had always admired something unique in her spirit. He'd been intrigued by her ambition, which was quiet yet consistent. The fact that she loved school and had been brave and determined when it came to firefighting.

Also, though she was a drama student, she was not a drama queen. In fact, she seldom complained, and he'd never seen her over-react. Rather, she was surprisingly calm.

"Why did you choose drama in school?" he asked.

"Well…" Jen hesitated and then it came out. All about her mother's penchant for "drama" and its effect on her and Teresa. "A counselor in high school suggested that I might feel empowered by acting in an appropriate situation—on stage. One thing led to another. And it is empowering. I know that there's no temptation in me to make a scene for attention or to manipulate people. I'm lucky. I don't have to fight it, because there's simply no urge to behave that way. Nonetheless, I'm still more like my mother than I want to be."

"I've met her."

"Yes." Her mother had been between lovers long enough to visit Santa Barbara and try to run her daughters' lives all those years ago.

"She didn't seem that bad. Were there ever any repercussions for her?"

"For telling lies and pretending she was afraid for her life? No. Not really. Certain people—neighbors, friends—stopped taking her seriously. That would have been a problem if any of us had actually ever been in danger, but of course we weren't. She was the woman who cried wolf. Still, she's not that way all the time. When she has enough going on in her own environment, she doesn't have so much time and energy left to try to control the rest of us."

"Control?"

"Oh, yes." Jen nodded emphatically. "Oversee, overprotect, supervise, observe, control. All of it. So," she finished very deliberately, "a little break is good for all of us."

"Does she try to control Elena?"

"In a way. The dynamic is different there, and they seem more able to be friends. But, then, Elena doesn't have a lot of independence yet."

"Is your mother suspicious of me?"

"My mother? Yes. Or she wants to be—or pretends to be. Whatever it is, she's doing it for her own ends. Whatever they are." *Sometimes,* Jen wanted to add, *I wish her act was supposed to benefit me.* But it would always be for Robin.

PETE, THEIR computer animation tech, had gone to school with Max. They'd been roommates in their undergraduate years. A rangy Long Island native, Pete had been into film and computers forever. He had a gift for visual art and had sold massive oil paintings to corporations who hung them in the lobbies of their head offices. He'd also been an excellent surfer, and Max couldn't count the hours they'd spent together floating in channel water dotted with tar, spotting dolphins, whales and so much more.

Pete picked them up in a Suburban he used for transporting sound equipment. One of his assorted money-making enterprises was handling sound for concerts.

The Colorado group climbed into the SUV, Bob and Pete in front, Max and the Delazzeri sisters in back, and headed south.

Teresa seemed to withdraw as she gazed at oil rigs, at the palms outside the Belmont in Montecito, at avocado trees, at all the things that spoke of Santa Barbara, of a life they'd shared so long ago. She sat by a window, with Jen in the middle and Max on Jen's other side.

"It's so beautiful," Jen said. "I forget. Or—well, I don't forget. I just…don't think about it."

Like Max, she'd spent much of her life by the ocean, but for her it was Monterey first, and then Santa Barbara.

"I picked up your bike from your dad's house, like you said," Pete tossed over his shoulder.

"A bicycle?" Jen asked. They'd all loved to ride when they were in college.

"Uh…no."

"Not a motorcycle?" Her horror couldn't have been more pronounced or instantaneous.

He grinned. "I wear a helmet."

"Lovely." Her jaw had tensed. "Elena wouldn't ride on it even if I allowed it. Which I won't, incidentally."

"I've noticed her extreme caution. But Elena isn't the passenger I was hoping for."

He wondered if she'd heard him. She peered out Teresa's window, and all Max could see was the perfect curve of her jaw.

"Your dad asked when he's going to see you," Pete continued.

"Not today."

"I said that was probably the case; that we planned on going straight to Canyon Wind Estates, straight to the house there."

Beside Max, Jen asked Teresa, "Are you okay?"

"Yes."

THE SUBDIVISION HAD BEEN well-planned—
but for the danger of fire. Eyeing the adobe
dwellings built on the California Mission
theme, Jen said, "I forgot how nice these
houses are." Max bit back the reply he was
tempted to make. A subdivision built on a
southwest-facing slope. It *should* have burned.

But Jen knew that, too. And Max had certainly made the point in conversation with
her.

Their rental house was two-storey, built
around a red-tiled courtyard replete with
planters and fountains.

"Everyone has his own room," Pete said.
"Unless people *want* to share." His eyes fell
upon Max and Jen, and Jen looked taken
aback. Max watched Pete's slow grin at this
reaction. Pete enjoyed baiting people he
believed to be overly serious; in Jen, he'd
found a new target. Well, she could take care
of herself.

Pride, he thought. Pride would have
made her especially prickly, if someone
suggested she'd be sleeping with *him.*
Because they had been lovers, he'd rejected
her, she'd borne his child and she would

never forget the smallest detail of the pain he'd caused her.

As they went through the house, choosing their rooms—although Pete had already selected a downstairs suite with plenty of shade so that he wouldn't have to keep the blinds drawn while he was on the computer.

Jen decided on a room upstairs, one with a four-poster bed and an outside sleeping porch. Teresa chose a corner room, looking away from Makal Canyon. Max took the front room beside Jen's. His was the master suite, off the sleeping porch. Bob's bedroom was across the courtyard from Max's, connected by an upper walkway.

Sitting on his bed, Max gazed through the wide French doors at the canyon where Salma died.

He thought of Jen, wondering why he'd taken the room next to hers. It wasn't because it was the master suite—or for the memory foam mattress he felt beneath the spread.

Why did I even ask her here?

She was going to help him with the documentary. She would interview subjects. She would use journalists' instincts he suspected she deliberately kept sheathed. She didn't want to be a rebel. She wasn't inclined to expose error or injustice.

I should have asked someone else to do this.

Why had he asked Jen? Because of Elena? So that he would have a chance to spend more time with his daughter and know her better? He could have done that in any case.

Because he'd used Jen to deal with Salma's death, her horrible death?

Use… He'd thought a lot about that word since he'd learned that a child had resulted from the week he and Jen had spent together making love. Had he used her? Had he ever used any woman?

Whatever his intentions had been back then, that week after the fire, they'd been neither pure nor mature. They had been… momentary. Gratuitous?

When he remembered, he didn't like himself all that much. The man he'd become did not treat women so callously. Max knew that lovemaking frequently resulted in one party or the other falling in love. So he didn't do that much of it and was selective. A woman had to be able to handle *his* independence, which meant having some of her own. That was the only way he stood a chance of falling in love. There'd been a woman smoke jumper years ago in Alaska. Which was why he'd left Alaska. He'd run into her on one fire since then. She'd married someone else and he'd been happy for her, but also sadder than he'd expected to be. He hadn't wanted to marry her, he'd left their relationship; and yet he had missed being with her.

Now, he had asked Jen Delazzeri here.

Okay, he'd been *attracted* to her when he was engaged to Salma. That wasn't a crime.

Once he'd seen her through her window next door—from the window of the room where he and Salma slept. Jen hadn't been undressing but standing in front of the mirror, doing ballet exercises.

She was too curvy for a ballerina, he had thought.

He'd made himself *not* look, not even glance toward that window.

But he couldn't forget. He'd never been able to forget, and whenever he'd seen her afterward the memory was there.

Until the fire.

Till Salma was burned.

Then… It just *happened.*

The world's most frequent and least explanatory excuse for all the errors of flesh in this world.

Error?

Disloyalty to his fiancée, who was injured, then dead.

Teresa had told him that Salma was dead. Teresa had been the one to call him on the phone, and she'd barely been able to speak. *Max, Max, you have to be with someone. You're with the Hotshots, right? You're with everyone?*

He'd been with one of the other guys when Jen had brought him the phone, turned and started to walk from the room, paused briefly at the door, walked out, making some decision to give him privacy. And then had changed her mind.

She'd come back.

She'd come back because they'd shared the shelter.

And after Teresa had told him, Jen and Jarod had sat on each side of him, had held him, and others had trickled in. People crying. Everyone crying.

He hadn't cried.

He'd never cried.

He'd had nightmares and been awakened from them by Jen. But that was later… Just a little bit later.

Strange that the memory of those nightmares, and awakening and finding her there brought him pain that seemed greater than Salma's death, which had been a numbness. Grief that wasn't exactly felt, but was more than felt.

It was after he'd overheard some of the other hotshots talking about the two of them that he'd said those things to Jen, whatever they were; the things he'd said before he'd left to join a hotshot crew in New Mexico. When he'd returned to Santa Barbara, Jen and Teresa were both gone, and that, he'd thought, was best.

He hadn't enjoyed his memories of the time he'd spent with Jen. Rather, he'd felt guilty, hating himself for how much he wanted her. Not even taking the time to get to know her the way he would have…if things had been different. Everything.

First Salma's pregnancy.

Then, he'd made Jen pregnant. He should have used a condom. He shouldn't have been selfish.

But he was.

That selfish man was still inside him. Parts of a person didn't evaporate. They came along for the ride, maybe partly transformed but still there. But he'd matured, and now he felt shame, and he couldn't undo who he'd been that year, that summer, that week.

His thoughts turned from fire to what he'd begun to think of as the Other Task. Telling his father about Elena.

His sisters would welcome their new niece, he knew. His father would, too, eventually.

Pete had told Norman Rickman that Max wouldn't be by that day. So maybe this was the day to surprise him. He could take the bike out.

Get away from Jen.

From what he felt, whatever that was.

He'd seen another helmet outside, with the bike, but he'd brought along his best one from Colorado. Little though he wanted to on such a clear summer day, he dressed in his bike leathers and left the room.

Jen was just coming out of hers, in blue jeans and a tank top. "Can't wait to risk your life, I see."

"Want to go for a ride?"

"No."

"Not even to dinner?" A postponement of whatever scene awaited him at the family home.

"I…" she lowered her voice slightly "…I'm not sure I should leave."

Teresa.

"I think she'd want you to. She's stronger than you give her credit for being."

"What do you know about it?" Her whispered retort was indignant.

"Tell her we're going for a motorcycle ride."

Jen's eyes wandered up and down his frame, but without any apparent approval. "I don't have the clothes for it."

"Did you bring a fire suit?"

"Of course not. I'm not signing up to be in another fire."

"I'll lend you some clothes."

"Like they'll fit!"

"You want to go, don't you?" He couldn't keep from grinning. "There is another helmet here. Let's see what we can find you in the way of protective clothing."

Her cheeks had turned pink, and Max thought of Elena's insistence that her mother still carried a torch for him.

Max wondered if Elena was right.

CHAPTER EIGHT

"OF COURSE YOU SHOULD GO," Teresa said. "I'm fine. You should take advantage of being away from Mom. You want the jacket?"

"Mom doesn't run my life," Jen replied. "You know that. I don't let her. And besides, it's *your* jacket."

"It's *ours*. But if Mom was here," Teresa said, her words seeming less slurred, more decisive than they had in months, "she'd be *warning* you. Which you don't need." Without asking, she went to the closet, removed a black leather jacket and pressed it on her sister.

Jen laughed. "No, I don't need to be *warned*."

Max stopped in the doorway of Teresa's room and saw the two sisters, catching that bright, sudden smile that he associated with the real Jen Delazzeri.

Jen wore Levi's and a long-sleeved T-shirt stamped with the logo of the Martial Arts Center, Lodo. As he watched, she pulled on a black leather jacket with plenty of zippers. On the back was a painted image of the street urchin from *Les Miserables*.

"If my jacket doesn't come back intact," Teresa told Max, "you're in trouble."

He winked at her. "I'll take good care of the jacket."

Teresa said, "I won't wait up."

As he and Jen walked down the wide tiled staircase, Jen said in a low voice, "She made a joke. She hardly ever jokes."

"She wasn't joking."

Jen rolled her eyes. "About the jacket. She loves this jacket. Actually, she and Mom and Elena and I saw the play on a trip to New York, and Mom got someone to airbrush the jacket for me. They didn't want to, because of copyright, and so forth, so she told them I was in the cast." She shook her head. "*Not* one of my prouder moments. I was mad, so I gave it to Teresa, who loves it. But she refuses to accept it as *hers*."

"And I think you love it, too," Max said knowingly.

"A bit." She smiled, half reluctantly, but the Jen he remembered—and cared for, maybe more-than-cared-for—reappeared like the sun peeking from behind a cloud.

MINUTES LATER, they were headed north and into the Santa Inez Mountains. Jen knew without asking where he was taking her, where they would eat. Cold Springs Tavern. They'd gone there as a group, as hotshots, on bicycles, riding up the pass from school. They'd played the jukebox, shot pool, danced.

Friends.

Hiking in the mountains.

It had been like family, a new and different family from the one with which she'd grown up. Despite her initial doubts, she loved being on the back of Max's motorcycle again. They'd traveled this way during the week that followed the fire. Down to the beach. Up the coast to another spot, where the Chumash Indians had left handprints in the stone on a high cliff. Magic everywhere.

Except that Salma had been dead, and Max hadn't talked about it; wouldn't talk about it.

As they crested the ridge of the mountain

range, Jen gazed out at the ocean, the oil rigs, everything. She had changed so much from the woman she'd been in college. She remembered, most of all, a vulnerability that, although not entirely vanquished, had been hammered into something stronger. Yes, she could fall in love. But her experience as a Muay Thai fighter, in particular, gave her a focus outside her inner tenderness. Her exterior was strong, had known pain, had fought and triumphed. Her spirit grew from her martial arts practice.

I want to go down to the beach, she thought, and she wanted to surf again, do all the things she had done growing up. When she was young, she'd danced and surfed in Monterey, the two things combined for her. She'd surfed with Teresa usually; neither of them wanting to surf with boys, both anxious in a rough-and-tumble world from which their mother had been so determined to protect them. Maybe Robin's protectiveness had helped lead Jen to martial arts; or maybe it was the drama of the spectacle. She had fallen in love with the most brutal fighting style, had even been to Thailand once, for two weeks of intensive study.

Yet people who didn't know her well perceived her as vulnerable. Jen hated this.

How did Max see her?

As she'd predicted, Max took them to the Cold Springs Tavern, and Jen found it largely unchanged, with a line of motorcycles parked outside beneath the evergreens, the air less dry than Colorado—and familiar.

She climbed off the bike, avoiding the hot tailpipes, and removed her helmet. A cool breeze lifted her hair, blowing dark tendrils back from her face. Max grinned at her as he pulled off his helmet. "You look the same," he said, as he had before.

"Thank you," Jen said. *I suppose.* "I'm not the same, though."

"Yes, so you've said." Again, a rather impish grin.

"I can't escape the feeling that you're— well, paying attention to me simply because I'm Elena's mother."

"Since I'm her father and I find you attractive and interesting, I can think of worse reasons."

Jen considered. So could she. "You don't know enough about who I am to find me interesting."

His eyebrows drew together slightly in puzzlement. "Are you always this inviting on dates?"

Jen laughed, surprising herself. "No. I'm hard on you."

"Let's have some dinner. To start your birthday celebration."

Her birthday was the following day. She'd told him the date not long before. And he'd remembered.

THE WOOD INTERIOR was rustic, the bar in one room, the dining space in another. As their waitress seated them at a table with a red-and-white checked cloth, they could hear the jukebox playing Lynyrd Skynyrd.

Jen chose the special, a sautéed duckling with wild greens. Max had seafood, and they shared their entrees with a glass of chianti each. Jen watched their candle flicker in its glass holder, wishing she could find it as easy to love and to trust as she had thirteen years earlier.

Yet she'd felt an excitement, a warmth of skin and limb and flesh as she pressed close to Max on his motorcycle. It wasn't his looks—though there was nothing to complain about in that regard. Age had given his face character, and she suspected he would grow even more attractive in the coming decades.

"Is your family looking forward to meeting Elena?"

Max lifted his head, brown eyes flitting to hers then back to his meal. "Now that you mention it…"

Jen waited.

He sipped his wine.

"I haven't told them yet."

She tried to remember his sisters, and she decided *they* couldn't be the ones he was uneasy about telling.

She played through the questions she might ask: *Why not? When are you planning to tell them?*

But of course he planned to tell them, because he'd promised Elena she would meet them.

"You wanted to do it face-to-face," she said.

"Yes."

"That makes sense." But sense wasn't what it made. She couldn't draw conclusions. She'd met Max's family, yet she remembered little about them. His mother had died when he was a teenager; his sisters were healthy and blond and fond of Max. His father was a doctor…. "Your father." Jen hesitated. "You were close to him, I remember."

No response.

"Are you still?" she asked.

"Well, I'm the only son. He's a physician. I'm a smoke jumper and a forest-service ranger."

"He's disappointed?"

"Yes."

"How do you think he'll react to learning you have a daughter? He won't reject Elena, will he?" It annoyed her to think that Elena believed finally knowing her father would be the answer to all her prayers and a salve for all her wounds. Nonetheless, she'd derive no satisfaction from watching her daughter be hurt by Max's father or siblings.

"No. I can't imagine that. He won't be happy with me, though."

Trying to predict what form his father's displeasure would take was impossible, Jen decided. Impossible for her, anyhow.

As long as he doesn't hurt Elena's feelings.

"What's our plan," she asked, changing the subject, "for investigating the fire?"

"We want to interview the principals, particularly on camera."

"Who else?"

"Some experts on wildland fire and on the problems with urban-wildland interface."

In other words, problems that occurred where privately owned land and structures met public lands.

"Are you planning on talking to home owners and prospective home owners in this, addressing how people can protect their homes in a fire season?"

"Yes, actually, and also urging buyers and developers to look carefully at wildfire danger before developing risky areas."

"Are you thinking about putting Teresa on film?" Jen asked. For her, the subject was a sensitive one. On film, Teresa's instability would likely be apparent. Jen didn't want her sister to see herself that way.

"I don't know yet. I want her to walk the ground with us. It could be useful to have her perspective, as someone who was there."

Teresa had the right to make her own decisions about something as important as this, Jen knew. To prevent her from choosing was to behave as Robin sometimes had in their lives, overly protective and controlling.

"When do you plan to start looking at the topography?" Jen asked.

"Tomorrow. Ideally, I would have liked to begin shooting the documentary on the nineteenth, the same day we arrived on the fire. But as it is, we're pretty close. And fortunately, there are photographs of the actual blaze."

"Do you think of the day of the blowup…" Jen stopped.

"What?"

She didn't know what had driven her to ask something so insensitive. She shook her head.

"Yes, for me, Salma died that day. It was the last day I saw her, and I didn't think she was going to make it. Neither did Richard. He told me so. He said to prepare myself."

Teresa had sustained minor burns in the fire, and she had been taken out by chopper with Salma. And Teresa had been at the burn center with Salma when Salma had died. She'd learned of Salma's death almost at once.

"No," Jen said. "She wasn't dead for you. Not until you learned she'd died."

"True, but I think of her death day as the day of the blowup."

Jen wanted to get away from the morbid conversation; wanted to get away from an irrational sense of her own responsibility. In no way had she caused or contributed to Salma's death. She hadn't even coveted Salma's fiancé. What had happened between her and Max...

But she didn't like herself when she remembered that time. Remembering made her culpable, as culpable as Max, in a mutual seduction or submission to attraction and to perilous circumstances. How could she blame Max for saying that it was all about the fire? Anyone, even the virgin she had been, should have guessed as much.

She'd wanted to think he was in love with her. In blaming Max for engaging in a casual, gratuitous affair without thought of the consequences, she had to admit her own part— which hadn't been so different. She'd been opportunistic, at the least.

Max's grief had been what she'd needed, perhaps. An excuse for intimacy with a man she knew like a brother, someone both attractive and familiar, known.

But she'd never really known him until she'd known him as a lover, and then she still hadn't known him, because he hadn't spoken about feelings that were locked inside, feelings about Salma's death.

"What are you thinking?"

Would it be mature, the mature thing, she wondered, to tell him the truth?

But what did she want now, and how would telling him the truth impact on her goals?

A voice within her whispered that she wanted Max Rickman's love. Not because she loved him, but because he hadn't loved her when Elena was conceived. And that was a completely childish desire.

"I was thinking about—what happened between us. After the fire," she admitted. "I keep blaming you and it's not fair, because I knew your girlfriend had just died. I took advantage of you, as much as you did of me."

Max lifted his eyebrows. "That's a new and interesting take on it."

"Isn't it," she agreed.

"I'd been attracted to you," he said, "before Salma died. To be honest, I'm attracted now."

The words thrilled her, a warm brush against her skin, a wind promising a future in which she wanted to believe.

But then it was gone more quickly than it had arrived.

"I'm not the same person," she said.

"The same thing is happening in me."

"Which is?"

"I want to know about you. I'm curious. You're mysterious to me. And I think that however well I know you, that will continue to be true."

Jen didn't answer.

What if she wanted more than to know the satisfaction of Max being in love with her? What if she wanted him to be in love with her for different reasons than she'd first believed?

"I'm *over* you," she said. "You can't seriously believe that after thirteen years I'd still be carrying a torch for you. You can't believe that of all the men in the world I'd have anything to do with you romantically. I mean, there's a lot of water under that bridge. And you probably feel as you do," she said, "because of Elena."

"What I said has nothing to do with Elena. But since you brought her up…"

She waited.

"She'll be coming out. I've bought the tickets, and she and your mother said it was all right and that they'd cleared it with you."

"Yes, yes." She turned her attention to her

food. She felt no particular distrust of Max. But she didn't understand where he was going with this conversation about her being mysterious. She set down her fork and demanded, "You don't think I'm going to sleep with you, do you?"

He reached for his wineglass and took a quick gulp. With a small smile, he resumed eating.

"You conceited…"

He shook his head.

Why was she always acting this way with him, to return again and again to the nineteen-year-old she'd been? Almost all her reactions to him were uncharacteristically immature, not to mention based on fear. Other men didn't affect her this way. At the martial arts center, she sparred with both men and women.

"So," he said, "Thai boxing."

As though following her thoughts.

"What about it?"

"You hurt each other. You have bruises."

She'd worn long sleeves every time she'd been near him. "Did Elena tell you this?"

"Yes. She thinks it's strange that you like to fight so much. She said you're 'scary,' but I think it was a compliment."

"Have you ever studied any martial art?"

"Only what Richard taught some of us." His voice was bitter as poison. "He didn't make me a fan of Oriental philosophy."

"I don't think of Muay Thai as having much to do with Oriental philosophy. Some, yes. But mostly I consider it an effective fighting art. There are others, but this is my favorite."

A slow smile. "Then what Elena says is true. You like to fight."

"In the ring. In the context of sport, yes."

"I'd like to see you do it."

"Really?" She didn't know why this surprised and pleased her—except that she *was* a decent competitor.

"Really."

"Maybe back in Colorado," she said.

"Do you practice on your own?"

"Yes, but that's not exactly a spectator event."

"Ah."

"This seems as good a time as any to ask why you blame Richard Grass for the blowup—or for the disaster it became."

"Because of where he put the crew on the east flank. And we were in the same danger. He's still in fire, Jen, and he's still screwing up."

She lifted her eyebrows and took a sip of her wine.

"Last year. Wyoming. A hotshot crew he was supervising nearly got trapped while doing a burnout. Which was, once again, a wrong decision."

A burnout, Jen knew, was a fire set inside a control line—a constructed or natural barrier to fire—to consume fuel between the edge of the fire and the control line. She wanted to believe Max; wanted for him to be right. But beneath his accusations against their former superintendent were emotions, some need for revenge. Maybe Max hoped, in some way, to undo Salma's death or right the wrongness of it by making someone acknowledge error.

The biggest error, in Jen's opinion, was the decision to build the Canyon Wind Estates—location. The second biggest error was choosing to risk lives defending those homes.

But she had friends in Colorado who built dream homes against the national forest. They made all the right sounds of acceptance about the possibility of loss. But this summer, when homes had actually been threatened, no one ever came out and said they didn't want firefighters to try and save the homes—even at the risk of their lives. She conveyed some of this to Max. "Where is Richard now, by the way?" she asked when they had finished their meal and were waiting for the check.

"Santa Barbara."

Jen blinked. "Now? During fire season?"

"He's a fire district administrator with the Bureau of Land Management."

"You want him fired, don't you," she said.

The waitress brought their check, and Max took the leather sleeve in which it had come and opened it. "Yes."

"I MISS THE OCEAN!" She yelled this through the wind, as they started down the highway. Unexpectedly, Max turned the motorcycle off their southeast course toward Carpinteria and down the winding Painted Cave Road that led toward Goleta. Toward the beach.

"I didn't mean now!"

He slowed and stopped, and she could see the lights of the oil rigs reflecting on the water below. "Do you mean," he replied over the idling engine, "that you *don't* want to go to the beach now? That you want to go home?"

She did want to go to the beach.

"It's okay," she said.

THEY TOOK OFF THEIR SHOES and walked on the shore outside the Belmont Hotel in Montecito. Jen had asked to go there because she didn't want to visit wilder shores she associated with their past. She didn't want Max to believe that her desire to see the ocean had anything to do with him.

Enjoying the water licking her toes, she said, "Our feet will be covered with tar."

"It doesn't hurt."

"No. It's worth it." Just to hear the splash of the water, the quiet rush of low waves, to feel wet sand under her toes. She wanted to cry, as if she'd suddenly been reunited with a part of herself she'd lost. Why had she ever left the ocean? Had she longed for mountains?

No. She had simply fled, determined to make a new life and become someone new— or rather accept that she was someone new. Maybe. Not a dancer anymore. No more fairy-tale dreams. Had she been hardened, disappointed by life?

But I love being Elena's mother. I've always loved it.

Max's arm reached around her shoulders, and she started, but he was merely steering her around a jellyfish that was lying on the wet sand.

Jen stopped to look at the jellyfish more closely in the moonlight and the lights from the concrete boardwalk. It glittered, iridescent, and she sat back on her heels and inhaled the scent of tar and saltwater, the combined unique smell of the South Coast. The heat, moisture, filled the backs of her eyes again.

"Happy birthday."

She blinked, stood up. Looked at him. "It's not midnight, is it?"

"No, but I thought I'd say it anyhow."

"Thank you."

She sensed Max watching her. What would happen if she looked up? Maybe he would think she expected him to kiss her. Not to look up, to keep walking, would reject the possibility, would kill the chance.

She wanted neither. Neither to eliminate the chance nor to encourage it—or seem to expect it. She said, "When are you going to see your family?" *And tell them about our daughter.*

"I'd planned to do it this evening, but it's late. After I take you back… Probably tomorrow," he answered at last. "Come on."

He took her hand.

His was large, hers small. Had he held her hand so long ago? Yes. He had done so many things right.

She allowed the touch, enjoyed it, enjoyed feeling his calluses, the integrity of a man who worked hard, who lived in the wild, who was somehow one with it. Someone who had become—in a fundamental way—the man he was supposed to be. Jen had not become exactly the person she'd once dreamed of being, and she could no longer even remember the dreams. She supposed they had involved fame, but as an actress or a dancer and not as a television news reporter.

Unexpectedly, surprising herself, she spoke honestly. "You make me feel young. It feels like, well, college."

"I feel that way, too," he responded in that deep, warm voice that she'd never forgotten. "But this is better."

"Is it?" She didn't pull her hand away. Why was he holding her hand? *Because of our child, that's why.*

A band was playing at a club across from the opulent Hotel Montecito, and Jen heard them doing a Pretenders song, "Brass in Pocket."

"Want to go dancing?" he asked.

"Now?"

"Not necessarily."

She glanced up and saw him watching her speculatively. "You smoke jumpers must be lonely guys," she said.

"What makes you say that? It happens to be true, but why did you say it?"

"Because…" She felt herself blush. Well, it was dark.

"Yes?"

"You seem to be almost pursuing me, and for the life of me I can't figure out why."

"Looked in the mirror lately?"

She shook her head, not to say that she hadn't looked in the mirror, but rather to indicate that she didn't buy what he said. "It's because of Elena, isn't it?"

"Try to remember that I asked you out to dinner before you told me about her. Is it such an alien thing for a man to pursue you?"

"No," she admitted. Perhaps he was sincere. Perhaps he simply found her attractive. Perhaps he had a few fond memories of the time they'd spent together in college and after the fire.

But she doubted it.

Yes, those could have been his reasons for asking her out to dinner the night they happened to run into each other on Silver Jack Ridge. *Happened to be in a burnover together for the second time of your acquaintance.* Yes, they'd had more intimacy than many people could count.

He released her hand, as if he sensed her reservations.

But she was wrong, because then he put his arm around her shoulders. "I'm attracted to you, Jen. Still, or perhaps I should say *again.* Or maybe it's something completely new. It feels new. Does it matter which it is? Not to me. I used to like you—I like you now. And I want to know what's made you so skeptical."

"You made me this skeptical." She spoke without thinking.

He dropped his arm from her shoulders. "Want to swim?"

"Tonight?"

He made a *tsk*ing sound in response. "Afraid of sharks?"

"No, and I'm not afraid of you, either."

When she glanced up, he was grinning, his teeth very white in the darkness.

"What?" she demanded.

"I think you are."

"That's the sort of vanity I should have expected."

But what she didn't expect, even after thinking he might kiss her, was his hand, almost trembling as it caressed her cheek. As he tilted her chin up and kissed her.

Her first thought was, *This could work.* Because she liked the kiss. It might just as well have been the first time. She could remember little of kissing him more than a decade before. His lips exerted a gentle pressure, his tongue drawing her forth rather than expecting or presuming.

Pulling back from Max, Jen met his eyes and said the last thing she'd expected to say, or even feel. "Thank you."

"Thank you," he replied, keeping an arm around her as they continued walking.

Yes, she'd dated since they'd last been together. *But this is different, Jen.*

How was it different?

She knew; knew with a rush of honesty so keen it hurt.

Going out on dates wasn't the same as becoming hopeful—hoping for more than a date, more than many dates.

For a deeper level of caring.

With Max, tonight in particular, she had begun to hope. And maybe to want.

She muttered, in irritation with herself, "I don't suppose you're frightened of *me?*"

"Terrified," he said, and she didn't know whether or not he was teasing. His arm stayed around her shoulders. "And with that admission—shall we head home?"

CHAPTER NINE

THEY FOUND THE OTHERS asleep. In dream-like privacy, Max kissed Jen good-night outside her bedroom door. And in the morning, when she awoke to a knock on the door she knew who was on the other side. She had slept in an oversized T-shirt with the cover of the vintage graphic novel *Tintin in Tibet,* on the back. "Come in," she said, drawing the covers up around her.

Max opened the door, saw her and stepped inside. He shut the door behind him and gave her an appreciative look.

Jen grinned. Didn't mean to, but couldn't help it. And remembered that this was her birthday.

Max didn't seem to remember or didn't mention it in any case. "I'm going to see my father this morning. Then I have an appointment with Richard. I wondered if you would mind killing an hour or so at a coffeehouse in Carpinteria, so that I can give my dad a chance to react without an audience. Then you and I can go see Richard."

It would keep him from making the long trip back to Canyon Winds Estates to pick her up.

"Sure," she agreed. "On the bike?"

"I thought so."

She didn't want to acknowledge how much she wanted to feel that closeness again, her front against his back, hugging his hard middle. "Okay. Give me a few minutes."

"Half an hour?"

She shrugged. "I don't need that long."

But she was glad to take it, glad for the time to take extra care with her makeup and the time to choose which top to wear with her blue jeans.

When they met in the kitchen, he had put on black leather chaps over his jeans. He scrutinized her jeans and said, "You should really have some of these, too."

Bob was at the table, sipping coffee with Teresa, and he gave Jen a speculative look.

"Riding motorcycles isn't normally a part of my life," Jen said. "I'm fine."

"Maybe it will be," Bob remarked.

Jen opened her mouth, then snapped it shut.

Teresa smiled. Strange, for years she'd looked sort of out of shape, pale and unaware. But already, after a night in California—and away from Robin, Jen thought—her color and her eyes were brighter. Like Bob, she seemed on the verge of openly teasing Jen and Max. "Happy birthday," she said.

"Thanks."

"How old?" Bob asked. "Or don't we ask that?"

"She's thirty-two," Max said.

He remembered that, at least, perhaps had thought about it.

Fifteen minutes later, she was clinging to him again, feeling like his girlfriend, while knowing she wasn't. He drove them into the town of Carpinteria, to a coffeehouse called Uncommon Grounds, and went inside with Jen. "I'm buying," he said, squeezing her hand briefly. "Your birthday coffee."

"Thank you."

"And it's a business expense."

"Did we say you were paying expenses?" Jen mused.

He gave her a wolfish grin, his eyes crinkling in the corners. "How do you think I'm going to talk you into letting me buy you motorcycle leathers to protect your precious skin?"

There was more in his words.

Skin.

Salma's skin.

Jackson's skin.

She lifted her eyes and saw that he wasn't smiling. Not sad, either. But serious.

"You may," she said. "You must have been saving your overtime for years."

"That's about it. Most important piece of smoke jumper equipment. That overtime book." He placed a hand on the middle of her back, guiding her ahead of him in the line.

Jen ordered a latte, and Max had black coffee. He sat with her at a round table for two on the patio, with a view over traffic, of the ocean and the oil rigs.

"Missing Colorado at all?" he asked, looking preoccupied.

"Are you kidding?" She shook her head. "I want to dive into that water. I'd like to swim with dolphins again." Maybe that was a bit of an exaggeration, but she'd lost count of the times during her life in California that she looked up in the surf to see the dorsal fins of passing dolphins or a whale's tail waving on the horizon. "What about you?"

He shook his head. Still with that preoccupied look, he said—almost to the sea rather than her— "It seems as if we were meant to be back here together." Then, he met her eyes. "Don't you think?"

She couldn't think. She could only feel. Her blood raced, and she remembered kissing Max the night before—and also Elena's pointed suggestion. *I am still attracted to him. More than attracted. And I want him to be more than attracted to me.*

"Maybe," she murmured, more to herself than to him.

Max grinned, that wolfish grin.

Jen decided to change the subject. "How will your father take it?" she asked at last.

That sobered him. He shook his head ruefully. "He has very high standards for the behavior of his children. Initially, he'll be disappointed in me. Unlikely he'll take it out on you or Elena."

Jen considered this. "What did he think of Salma? Did he know she was pregnant?"

"Negative—no, that is. He thought I was

too young to get married. On one occasion, he referred to her as 'a bit of fluff.' "

"Should I look forward to a similar reception?"

Max shook his head. "Granted, he probably won't be keen on the fact that we met, let alone conceived a child, while we were hotshots together."

"What does that have to do with anything?"

"It's where I went wrong, according to him. Left the career track."

"As I recall, your course of study wasn't exactly 'career track,' though I'm not sure what that means."

"Being on a career track, in his mind, means not fighting wildland fire for a living. If I could find it in myself to become a fire chief, he would find that easier to live with, I think."

Jen gave that some thought. "He's a physician?"

"An orthopedic surgeon."

"A holy calling," she murmured and realized that it maybe sounded a bit sarcastic. Becoming a physician took an enormous amount of study and dedication. But Jen heard the frustration in Max's voice, because his father would not accept him as he was. *I hope I'm never that way with Elena, wishing her to be different than she is.*

"He wanted me to go to medical school, too. In fact, he wanted that from all of us."

"Did any of you oblige?"

He shook his head. "I think we all resisted doing the thing that would instantly have meant, all by itself, instant respect. From him. It's strange, because we all admire the hell out of him. Maybe we thought that no matter *what* we did we'd never be good enough." He drained his coffee. "Can you keep busy for an hour and a half?"

"Sure. I might walk around town a bit, but I'll be back here at ten-thirty."

"Good, our appointment with Richard is at eleven."

"Is he expecting both of us?"

"No. Don't worry. Your presence will make him feel better. In fact, I'm sure he'll be glad to see you."

"Why are you so sure of that?"

"Look, he'll be glad to see *anyone* who isn't me."

"Did you have words after the fire?" Jen squinted, trying to remember what she knew.

"Oh, yes. I'll tell you about that later."

As Max headed for the oceanfront house where he'd grown up, Richard Grass was the last thing on his mind. All he could think about was what words he would use to tell his father about Elena. All he could do was try to second-guess his father's reaction so that he could have the best possible response ready.

The house was a white stucco Mission-style, with wrought-iron appointments and a tile roof. From the road, Max could see the top of the railing on the stairs leading down to the beach. Every morning in his teens, he'd gone down to the water with his surfboard and his sister Marina, a stack of toast in his free hand. His father had never been slow to remind them that his hard work and their mother's careful financial management had provided this environment for them. Max stifled a sigh as he parked his bike behind a blue-gray Toyota hybrid. That would be his father's car.

We have a good relationship, Max reminded himself.

But that relationship would always be limited by his father's unmet expectations of his only son.

And having fathered a child out of

wedlock was not going to improve Max's stock with Norman Rickman.

The front door opened, and his father stood there. Rangy and broad-shouldered like Max, his father now had a wild mane of white hair, its tousled character at odds with the person Max knew him to be. He wore tennis whites and waved to Max, coming down the front step and across the wide lawn, walking on the flagstone path.

Max removed his helmet and set it on the handlebars where it rested securely. He climbed off the bike. "Hi, Dad."

They embraced, and his father said, "You look fit. How are those knees holding up?"

"Not too well," Max admitted. "I'm looking for something on the ground next season."

"I thought you smoke jumpers would rather go out in wheelchairs than voluntarily give it up."

"Not this smoke jumper."

His father seemed to approve of this response. "Misty is going to come over later today. She's looking forward to seeing you."

"I'm looking forward to seeing her, too, but I can only stay for about an hour right now. I have an appointment in connection with the film."

"I'm glad you're making that film," his father said. "Maybe it will get that fire out of your system once and for all."

He'd been unfair to his father. He'd forgotten that his dad knew what a huge event the Makal Canyon tragedy had been in Max's life. He'd forgotten that his father had always understood more about his children than most other people did.

I'm dreading his reaction. That's why I was unfair.

"Want some water or tea? Orange juice? Coffee?"

"Thanks, I'm fine."

"Thought we'd sit out on the patio."

"Sounds great."

There, the smell of beach tar brought the past even closer—and not just the distant past. There was last night. And there was this morning, too, with Jen clinging to him as they rode on his motorcycle.

He sat across from his father, wondering how to say the impossible. Finally, he said, "Well, I've had a shock recently."

He felt his father's sudden alertness and tension and he realized at once that a parent's immediate concern would be for his child's health.

It was this, his father's fear, the fear of a man who'd lost his wife to cancer, that made Max hurry on. "I've just learned that I have a twelve-year-old daughter."

He was glad for his father's healthy blood pressure, like Max's own. He told himself there was no danger of a coronary.

"Are you sure it's yours?"

Max heard those words echo with the pull of the waves, synchronous. "It?" he said in disbelief.

"I'm sorry. I didn't mean that."

"She," Max said with subtle emphasis, "looks like Misty. Her name is Elena. And yes, I'm sure. Her mother is Jen Delazzeri."

"Twelve. When did this… Not that it's any of my business."

Right.

"Who is… What did you say her mother's name is?"

Max repeated it. "She was a Santa Inez Hotshot."

"Well, that's certainly followed you like wake follows a boat."

His father's reaction seemed slightly better

than Max had anticipated. It was a relief, he found, to talk to him about this.

"Why are you only finding out now?" Norman Rickman suddenly demanded.

Max was unsure how to respond. He no more wanted Jen to be the object of his father's scrutiny than he wanted to feel the man's censure himself. How best to protect Jen?

The truth. After all, weren't her doubts the results of your behavior?

On the other hand, some of it was too personal to share with his father.

"Salma's death," he improvised. "It's not that simple. She was uncertain how I would react."

"Every woman is uncertain how a man's going to react to her pregnancy," his father exclaimed.

Max had forgotten this side of his parent. That Norman Rickman could be defensive if he believed someone had wronged one of his children. He would defend them, no matter who was to blame. Sometimes.

And Jen did wrong you, Max.

To have been given the chance to see Elena born, to see her nurse or take her first steps… What part would he have played, in reality? *I would have been there. At first, I might have had doubts. But I would have taken part. And I would have loved Elena from the moment I saw her.*

Just as he had upon meeting her when she was twelve. She was his blood.

But he wasn't going to hold that against her mother, now. What was the point? Done was done, and now he could only make up for lost time. And he wanted that time with both of them. Jen fascinated him. He wasn't sure why, what it was about her, but he knew what it meant. He could get in over his head.

He didn't care. He was a smoke jumper and he dropped through the air for a living. He could handle whatever came along with being close to Jen Delazzeri. And he believed those things would be good, in any case.

"So what are your plans," his father asked, "regarding this child?"

The rhythm of the ocean played against the light breeze that lifted Max's hair.

Strange. He'd been worried that he wouldn't be able to live up to his father's expectations about what a parent should be or do. But now that didn't concern him at all. The fear was gone because being a good father to Elena seemed the most natural course he could follow. There was no way he *couldn't* do this, no way he wouldn't. "To be the best father I can be," Max said.

"That's my boy."

Max could hardly understand why his father's praise still touched him so deeply. He was a grown man himself. Yet when Norman Rickman said that, he felt a foot taller.

"What about her mother?" his father asked.

"Working on it." Max smiled.

Norman nodded his approval. "Can't imagine a woman keeping that business to herself. Don't know what she was thinking."

Max did not agree. He knew. He had caused Jen's fear by saying that the love they'd shared had happened only because of the fire, only because of Salma's death. He'd hurt her. It would be chivalrous to drop a hint of this to his father, but right now he couldn't tell the whole truth. He said, "Dad, please don't be too hard on her. She saw how I was taking Salma's death."

"But why didn't she realize that a baby

would have been the very thing to help you recover from your loss?"

Salma's baby... Yes, she had been autopsied, but the pregnancy had been kept confidential. His father didn't know.

"I'd acted in a way that hurt her. That's all I can say. It was my fault." Not quite the entire story, but it might make his father more accepting of nineteen-year-old Jen's decision-making. *Fault?* He'd hurt Jen, but that didn't excuse her from not telling him about their child. "Also, remember that we were both very young—and that it's history now. We can only pick up from where we are."

"And she wants you to have a relationship with this child?"

"Only on our daughter's behalf. I think if it was up to her..." Max realized he'd spoken too freely. He wished he'd been less candid.

His father frowned. "Which one was she? Jennifer, did you say her name was?"

"She lived next door. She has long, dark hair. She was studying drama, dance, communications. Now she's a television newscaster."

"I remember her," Norman said thoughtfully. "I always thought she had more to her than Salma."

Max could not believe his father had actually said that. Salma had died, leaving grieving family and loved ones behind. Then he looked at his watch. "Well, I have an appointment—I should keep moving. I'll come by again."

"Surely you're not still emotionally involved in that death."

"I'll be emotionally involved in that death all my life," Max answered. Time had lessened the pain, as it would have any loss. Obviously, he was *over* what had happened. But because of it, he'd slept with Jen, and now there was Elena.

"Well, it seems to me you have other things to think about now," his father said.

"Actually, I'm thinking about them. This documentary. Better go."

His father walked him out to the front of the house.

"Where is she, by the way?" he asked Max.

"Who?"

"My grandchild."

Max's heart rushed, and he forgave the older man every negative word about Salma and her death. "Colorado. But she'll be out to visit soon. She's looking forward to meeting everyone."

UNEASILY, JEN FOLLOWED Max into the Santa Barbara offices of the Bureau of Land Management. She'd been pleased by Max's brief report of the meeting with his father. But the meeting that lay ahead of them now came with its own set of pitfalls.

She had liked Richard Grass. She'd admired him, been grateful for his encouragement when she was a rookie hotshot. Now, Max wanted to hang the blame for the Makal Canyon tragedy on him, and Jen wasn't particularly keen to be part of that process. And yet she knew she would be.

She'd spent her time at the coffee shop preparing questions for this meeting, but even as she did so she'd realized that a truly aggressive reporter would want to interview Richard for the first time in front of the camera, to give him no warning of the attack ahead.

Even so, her instinct *was* to warn him. Her instinct was to play good cop to Max's bad cop, and *never* to let Richard Grass be blamed in the film.

And she didn't understand her own feelings on the subject.

"We have an appointment with Richard Grass," Max told a ranger who was seated behind a counter, where glass display cases showed a mountain lion skull and a stuffed rattlesnake, as well as other natural artifacts.

Then he appeared. Dressed in a BLM uniform, still trim, unaffected by his confinement behind a desk, which Jen realized probably wasn't confinement after all. He was fighting fires in a leadership capacity. That was how she would approach the interview, she decided. It wasn't the strategy she'd planned, but it was natural and it might serve as a good neutral area between her own aims and Max's, which were not quite the same. He wanted Richard fired. Jen wanted only to know his part in the Makal Canyon fire—and in Salma's death and her own sister's consequent mental problems.

"Jennifer! You look wonderful. Unchanged."

"Oh, I'm changed," she said, laughing. "And I would say the same to you."

"Max," Richard greeted the former squad boss, shaking hands. "I hear you're smoke jumping."

"Possibly my last season."

"Let's go into my office."

It was a bachelor's office, without photos of wife or children. Instead, there were photos of Richard in *gi* and black belt, of Richard with his dogs, a pair of Akitas, one black-and-white, one brown-and-white.

Behind his wire-rimmed glasses, Jen thought his green eyes were wary. Did he know or guess Max's agenda?

Jen brought out her tape recorder. "May I use this?"

"Of course, of course," Richard answered uneasily. "But this is just a preliminary interview, right? And I want to offer my services for this documentary in any way I can. I'm happy to research old records or update you on changes in the way the BLM fights fires now."

He wanted to participate in the creation of the film. Jen had turned on the tape recorder. "Yes, it's just preliminary," she said. "And I'm sure—" she looked at Max, fairly certain that what she was about to say *wasn't* true as far as he was concerned "—we can use your help. Of course, I'm just the narrator."

"More than that," Max said, shifting his chair slightly closer to her, reminding her of their alliance. "Yes, we can use your help,

Richard. Thank you. There are questions only you can answer."

"I'd like to say what I think. And that's what the official fire investigation pointed out. The fire should have been suppressed much earlier."

"I'm interested especially," Max said, "in your decision-making regarding the deployment of our crews—particularly the crew on the east flank. But you actually had two crews cutting fire line downhill."

"Max, there simply wasn't another way to fight that fire. It's questionable if it should have been fought in those circumstances. In retrospect, I should have said, no, I wouldn't do it that way. I should have marched both groups down from those ridges. But we truly didn't know another way to stop the fire before it hit the Canyon Wind Estates. There were, as you know, certain similarities to the South Canyon fire. If we'd been able to study the lessons of that first fire, not yet prepared in official reports, we would have done things differently in Makal Canyon."

Jen gauged Richard's level of candor and found it surprisingly high. And yet he had become a bureaucrat. His official line, she saw, would be, *We do things differently now. Safety first. Always.*

What she wanted to know was the magnitude of any discrepancy between the official line and what had actually happened in the field.

"Tell me about your present responsibilities." Jen kept her tone deliberately friendly, nonconfrontational. "I think the viewers will be very interested in what you have to say about the fires of this summer."

"Fortunately, it's been a quiet season in this district. Not like you're having in Colorado."

The initial interview, an hour long, ended up veering, inevitably, into Richard's martial arts experience.

It was Max, who'd remained quiet and watchful through most of the meeting, who finally said, "Jen's a Thai boxer."

Richard blinked. "Now, that's a brutal sport for a man or a woman. Very effective."

"I don't know what it is, really," Max admitted.

"Boxers. With gloves, but they also kick, use elbow strikes, use basically everything at their command except the intentional awareness of *yin* and *yang*."

Jen couldn't smother a smile at Richard's

description, particularly the absence of that "awareness" which made aikido so effective. He was wrong about its absence in Muay Thai, anyhow. So many students of fighting arts believed their art superior to all others. She didn't feel this way.

The interview concluded with Richard taking their phone numbers, as well as directions to the place that was becoming known as "the fire house." He wanted to see Teresa again. "Poor kid," he said. "I worried about her. We were all over there together." On the east flank. "What's she up to?"

"Not what she planned on before the fire." Jen vowed to do her best to let Teresa explain herself. Or not. "Different things," she added, deliberately vague.

MAX SEEMED SUBDUED after the meeting. Maybe his wrath against Richard had diminished slightly. As they reached the motorcycle, Jen said, "What do you think?"

"About him?"

"Of course."

"A bureaucrat. Whatever he says, he's going to protect himself and the Bureau of Land Management. What do *you* think? About him?"

"Similar," she said.

Max handed her a helmet.

Climbing on the seat behind Max, Jen asked, "Home?"

"Actually, I thought we'd play for a couple of hours. Unless you're anxious to get back."

"There's work to do," she pointed out.

"It's your birthday." He turned the key in the ignition, then twisted around to see her face behind its shield, his own in similar shadow. "Okay?"

She felt her smile take over. She thought fleetingly of Elena and how since coming to California she herself had been less consumed by her daughter's life, more in tune with her own. "Okay."

CHAPTER TEN

HE TOOK HER to a Montecito shop that sold nothing but beautiful motorcycle leathers. There, he talked her into black leather chaps, a sexy and unnecessary but also unusually classy black leather halter-bustier, boots and a leather jacket, which the resident artist airbrushed with a wood hare, Jen's Chinese astrological sign. She left wearing all her new garments except the jacket—because it was warm out—and carrying everything else in an upscale shopping bag.

Out on the street, Max gently touched her bare upper arm to guide her across the drive toward the exquisite Hotel Montecito.

"What do we need over there?" she asked.

"Lunch. And something else." He stopped at a flower stand on the wide lawn and bought her a bouquet of lavender-colored roses.

"What do lavender roses mean?" she asked him.

"I don't know what the official line is."

"The unofficial, then?"

"That purple outfit you were wearing the day I met Elena. I like you in purple. Maybe it's *passion*."

They ate seafood for lunch, rode the motorcycle out onto the pier, then briefly went to the zoo. It was five when Max finally asked if she was ready to go home.

"How are you going to explain where we were and why we weren't working?"

"Oh, it will be obvious to everyone that I was working."

"On me," Jen said.

"Something like that."

THAT NIGHT, as Jen was getting ready for bed, there came a knock at her door. Jen went to open it and found her sister there, holding a small wrapped package.

"Happy birthday," said Teresa, stepping into the room.

Jen's new leather clothing lay over a chair near the foot of her bed.

"Thank you." Jen took the package, which had no card.

"So Max has just forgiven you," Teresa said, sounding almost disappointed by her sister's good fortune.

"And I him," said Jen, no longer certain that she wanted the package in her hands— or anything to do with Teresa's mood, with whatever was going on with her. She decided on a strategy of friendliness. Teresa, usually the gentlest of creatures, could be testy when she'd decided that Jen had done something that she, Teresa, would never do. "Richard's looking forward to seeing you."

"He was good to me," Teresa said. "I always liked him. Max is prejudiced against him, and he's trying to buy your allegiance." She gazed pointedly at the leather clothing draped over the chair.

Jen tried to deflect the insult. To not feel it *as* an insult. Max had bought her clothes because it was her birthday, because she was the mother of his child, because he liked her. "Should I have held out," she asked, "for candy or books?" Because he'd given her flowers.

"Well, he'll expect *something,*" Teresa

said. "But I doubt it's anything as mundane as sex."

Jen sat down on her bed, glanced at the package she held, then at her sister. "Is it safe to open this?"

Teresa said, "Of course. I couldn't afford anything like what Max gave you." She frowned at the lavender roses in a vase on Jen's countertop.

"Teresa, what's wrong?" Jen tried again.

"Absolutely *nothing*."

Sure.

"I'm sorry I was gone all day." Why, when Teresa behaved this way, did she respond by apologizing, even though she'd done nothing wrong?

"I wouldn't have come," Teresa said, "if I thought we were just here to promote your relationship with Max."

What an interesting remark. "That's not *why* we're here. And when we came... Look, he's Elena's father." Her protest trickled away, lame, sinking. "Did something happen today while we were gone?" she finally asked. "You weren't like this in the morning."

"Nothing happened."

"What did you do today?"

"I went for a hike."

"To the ridge?" Jen asked, already knowing the answer. Her sister had gone to the ridge where she and Salma and the others in their party had been trapped and overrun by flames.

"Of course. That's why I came here. To revisit that place. To remember, so that I can move on."

Jen was out of her depth. She was no counselor. Teresa was a psychiatric patient; she had a psychiatrist who was also her psychotherapist. "Have you called Dr. Malloy on your cell phone?"

"It's not up to you to suggest when I need to talk to my psychiatrist. My relationship with Dr. Malloy is private, none of your business."

Jen knew this to be true. However, she also knew that Teresa had been aggressive toward her, mean and challenging. Which made whatever was going on her business. "I'm sorry I wasn't here," she said, "to visit the place with you. If you feel like going back tomorrow, I'll be glad to come with you."

Teresa shrugged, and the accusatory storm seemed to have died in her. "Whatever," she said, almost indifferently, but the act didn't quite fool Jen.

Jen decided that attentiveness was the best gift she could give her sister at this moment. "Did it look the same?"

"No. I only knew it was the same place because of a boulder. There was this boulder that looked like a rooster, and it was still there, and it still looked that way. It looks over the place where we deployed shelters."

Jen wished she could give back to her sister everything Teresa had lost in the fire. But she had no power to undo the past.

She untied the ribbon on the package Teresa had given her.

"I got them in Denver," Teresa said as Jen lifted the lid on the small box. "I thought they'd match what you usually wear."

Earrings. The style was Art Deco, and they were purple, copper and black. "Thank you. They're really nice."

"Do you like them?"

"Yes. I'm going to try them on right now." Jen fitted the hoops through her ears and stood up to check the effect in the mirror.

Teresa said, "You look beautiful. You've always been the pretty one."

"That's not true," Jen said—and yet she knew that it was true, lately. Teresa's problems had affected her health and her looks. Once or twice, Jen had tried to interest her sister in going to the martial arts center. She'd been willing to take any class with Teresa, to study t'ai chi chuan or ju-jitsu or dance or anything that suited Teresa. But Teresa had always refused.

"Shall we go up to the ridge together tomorrow?" Jen asked. "Just the two of us? Gosh, I'm crazy about these earrings. They're gorgeous."

"I'm glad you like them. Sure, we can go tomorrow."

Jen hesitated. "Do you remember that day?"

"Yes. Not every detail, but I remember. Bob was talking about Jackson today, about hearing him scream."

Jen wondered if this was part of what had upset her sister. *I shouldn't have encouraged her to come.* She'd believed that bringing Teresa back to Makal Canyon would help free her sister from the past. But that wasn't what was happening.

I was a fool.

Or, more to the point, she'd been too concerned about what might happen between herself and Max and Elena to think effectively about Teresa's concerns. As of tomorrow, that needed to change.

Teresa suddenly grinned. "The new leathers look great on you. I would have accepted them, too, Jen. I was just in a snit."

"Thanks for saying that," Jen answered, "but I'm not sure you would have. You've always been more scrupulous than me."

"I think," Teresa said, "I'm just less sure than you of my own determination to do the right thing."

THE RIGHT THING. Jen's ideas about "the right thing" were shaped by Muay Thai and other fighting arts. Not abusing power. Protecting the weak. Integrity.

She wasn't sure where exposing wrongs that had occurred more than a decade earlier fit in. Also, with so much time passed and human memory inherently fallible, how was she to determine right from wrong?

She reminded herself that the mandate of the journalist wasn't necessarily to provide answers, so much as it was to ask the important questions. She could ask those questions without an agenda as to what the answers should be. Indeed, that was the only way to get at the truth.

Max's plan, going in with preconceived notions about what had happened thirteen years before, wouldn't necessarily lead them to the truth. Well, it might—but it could also lead them astray.

She and Teresa set out alone on their hike to the ridge where Salma had been burned. Max had asked where they were going, and Jen had replied, *To have girl time.* If Max accompanied them, it might well renew her sister's bad feelings of the night before.

The ridge was more than a mile from the Canyon Wind Estates. The summer morning was warm, though fog hung over the distant coast. The interior had grown uncomfortably hot by ten o'clock, making it too easy to remember the scorching heat of the day of the blowup.

"Is this hard for you?" Jen asked her sister. "To be back here?"

"No. One good thing is happening. I suppose that I've had survivor's guilt about Salma's dying, but being back here I remember things more clearly. Her fire shelter gusted up, you know. She'd deployed it at a bit of an angle."

That was important to know; it could influence how the fire was remembered and how Salma's part was remembered as well. Nothing about Salma deploying her shelter in a vulnerable position or in the wrong direction had been included in the report of the fire investigation. And such a thing could matter. Salma should have deployed the shelter so that her feet would be toward the blaze. If she hadn't, that could have helped to account for the severity of her burns.

"Of course we shouldn't have been there at all," Teresa added, "but that wasn't my fault, either."

"Whose was it?"

"Oh, Richard was the one who made the decision, along with some local BLM guys. I mean, Richard was responsible for us hotshots. We were his crew and his responsibility. I'm with Max on that."

"You know," Jen said, "since the South Canyon fire, hotshot crews and other firefighters have been saying no to building line down slope. They're taking responsibility for their own safety."

"That's where my guilt comes from, I suppose," admitted Teresa. "I think we *should* have said no. I should have. I'm an assertive person. I speak up when I think something's wrong. But that day I didn't. And I still don't know why."

"We were pretty young."

"You were. But I'd seen a thing or two, and I was getting ready to go to medical school. I think the fire showed me what a bad idea that would have been, for me to become a physician."

"Why?" Jen exclaimed. "That's nonsense."

"No, it's not. I knew we shouldn't have been building fire line downhill, but I listened to Richard's reasoning and went along with it. If you're a physician, you must never do that."

Jen felt keenly what a loss it had been to the medical profession that her sister, so wise *and* truly determined to speak the truth, had been deflected from the path. She tried to work out the best way to share her feelings with Teresa but she couldn't find the words. After all, it was too late for Teresa to turn back to that course, wasn't it?

But it wasn't too late for her sister to lead a productive, fulfilling life.

"Do you ever think," Jen asked tentatively, "of going back to school?"

"I've been going back to school for thirteen years," Teresa said tiredly. And it was true. "If I were to get a graduate degree now, it would be in sociology."

"To do social work?"

"Yes. To help the mentally ill as an advocate. But who's going to take me seriously, when I'm one of the multitude?"

Jen understood. Her sister's plight saddened her. "Do you think you became sick..." She hesitated over the word, hesitated after uttering it, checking to see how it was received. "Because of the fire?" she concluded at last.

"Oh, only in part." Teresa sounded even more weary. "Here. Here's the boulder."

It did, in fact, resemble a rooster. Jen had never been to this place, either before or after the fire.

"Where did you deploy your shelters?" She'd seen photographs and mechanical drawings—part of the fire investigation's official report, and so she thought she could find the place. But she wanted to see what Teresa remembered, *before* people like Richard Grass and Max came along to try to make her remember things differently.

Max had been to this place. He'd hiked

here as soon as it was safe for his group to leave their shelters.

Jen still wondered what he'd felt upon learning that while he'd been sheltering Jen Delazzeri, his fiancée had been burned so badly that she would die within twenty-four hours.

Teresa showed Jen where the shelters had been deployed, frowning as she tried to remember where each of her fellow hotshots had been. She could only remember three, including Salma.

They had all been overwhelmed by the extent of Salma's injuries.

"She wasn't closer to the blaze than anyone else," Jen pointed out. "So what you said, that her shelter came partway off her, must be the reason she was so badly burned." Though the day had now grown hot, she shivered. The same could have happened to her at the helicopter landing spot during the Silver Jack Ridge fire.

Fire had come inside her shelter.

But she'd been spared, unlike Salma.

Figures were walking toward them from the direction of Canyon Wind Estates. Jen recognized Max and Bob by the way each of them moved. After a moment, she realized that the third must be Richard Grass.

She wasn't made up to work, but Bob carried a camera. So maybe the viewer would simply hear her voice asking questions or not hear her at all for this segment. Richard Grass must be the intended subject today. He wore his Bureau of Land Management uniform.

Yes, the camera would be on him, and Jen didn't understand why she felt apprehension on his behalf.

"WE—DICK HENRY AND George Riley and I—discussed how best to fight the fire. We'd done an aerial observation together, and during the flight I pointed out that I never like to build fire line downhill."

"Pointed out?" said Max now, ironically. He, Jen, Bob, Teresa and Pete, the computer animation tech, were reviewing the footage of Richard Grass, who had since gone home.

"Don't be so judgmental," Teresa said.

"We're trying to make some judgments here," Max told her, rather sharply.

Jen eyed him, ready to warn him off if he made another similar outburst. But Teresa did not need her sister to fight for her. Teresa said, "Yes, but I don't think his word choice is really what you're trying to judge. You want to know who made the decision to build fire line downhill. He said Dick and George did."

"And George, conveniently, is dead." He'd had a fatal heart attack three years before.

They hadn't yet managed to contact Dick Henry, though they had tracked him down to his present home in upstate New York. But he was on vacation in New Zealand until mid-August. A spanner in the works.

The tape ran on a small monitor around which the five of them were now grouped. "I told them I didn't like it," Richard continued, "but George was IC, incident commander, and he made the call. He said there wasn't a good way to fight the blaze, but that this was the most efficient, given the conditions. I didn't disagree. Now, I know that I should have. Fortunately, the world of firefighting has been more forgiving of my error than I've been of myself."

"I can't stand the guy," Max said. "'Fortunately'? What exactly is that supposed to mean?"

"That he still has a job," Teresa said testily. "I'm going to bed." She stood up from the rocker behind Bob's chair. From there she'd remained slightly apart from the group, a separate entity with separate ideas.

Jen said, "Teresa, would you like to be interviewed outside tomorrow? We could go back to the rooster boulder. I think it might be good to have you talking about how you remember that landmark."

"That sounds fine." Teresa's voice, usually a bit sleepy and imprecise, was now firm.

As she left the room, Max stood up to follow her. Jen wondered what he intended to do or say, but decided that it was none of her business—and that Teresa could take care of herself.

"TERESA?"

Jen's sister glanced back down the stairs at Max. "What?"

"I'm sorry. I didn't mean to be…aggressive."

"Just remember," Teresa said, "that you weren't there. Not where we were. I know you want this documentary to reach certain conclusions, but you can't expect us all to do what you want just because you put this thing together."

Max was insulted. Did Jen think this was what he was doing, or was it only Teresa? "I want everyone to tell the truth," he said. "I just believe that Richard Grass isn't being truthful."

"If he's not," Teresa said, "and, by the way, I'm not saying for a minute that's the case, then it will come out. Maybe you should trust the process. Don't you think the documentary itself will reveal the truth, whatever that truth is?"

Max didn't answer. He stood barefoot on the tile floor, thinking about what Teresa had asked him. Did he think the documentary would reveal the truth? Yes. Unquestionably.

So why did he feel compelled to manipulate things? Unquestionably, he *did* feel that way. But even that question seemed one he couldn't ask without knowing the answer in advance. So he supplied his programmed answer. Richard Grass was a smart, charismatic man who could slant viewer response as he wanted, despite the best intentions of the filmmakers to discover the truth.

"Or is it," Teresa said, speaking from the shadows like the voice of his conscience, "that you don't really want to know the truth?"

"I want to know," he answered tersely.

From above, she said, "Good night then, Max. You'll hear part of it tomorrow."

Why should those words fill him with apprehension? Teresa would be before the camera. What truth did she know that might injure him?

CHAPTER ELEVEN

JEN'S CELL PHONE WOKE HER the following
morning. It was Elena. "Have you forgotten
I exist?" her daughter asked.

"No, I haven't. I tried to call you last night."

"When you knew I'd be at rehearsal."

"False," said Jen. "I thought yesterday was
a Tuesday. I was wrong."

"Well, guess what?"

"What?"

"About my trip out to see you on Friday."

"You can't come," Jen guessed.

"Grandma's coming, too. She bought a
ticket. She says you're allowing Max too
much power in my life."

This was outrageous. Jen lay in helpless
silence, aware of others moving about in the
hall. Probably Teresa waking up; Teresa,
who had agreed to go before the camera
today and talk about Makal Canyon.

"Is she there?" Jen asked. "You're calling from home. Is she there?"

"She's at yoga."

Yoga class. "She's already bought a ticket?" Jen said it in the hope that she'd somehow misheard her daughter.

"Alas. I think she's coming to teach you how to raise children without men. You've already learned that lesson."

"Your dad and I are *friends,*" Jen told her daughter, glancing toward the motorcycle leathers on her chair, remembering Max's hand on her bare back as they'd crossed the street together, with her in that black leather halter top—a garment that would certainly raise Elena's eyebrows. Most of all she remembered kissing him, and that there'd been no repetition of the experience the night before. "We've been riding around on his motorcycle together. We get along fine. I'm not committed to your grandmother's ideals, *if* raising children without male input is one of her ideals—which I'm not conceding, not for a moment."

"So, are you, like, *dating* my dad?"

"Not exactly."

"You're not sleeping with him, are you?" Elena demanded.

Jen hesitated. She certainly was not sleeping with Max. But it had never occurred to her that Elena might have any objections to that scenario.

"You are?" Elena sounded both disgusted and horrified.

"No. No, I'm not. I was just wondering why it would be such a big deal if I was."

"It's just that everything in the world," Elena said, "isn't about you. Whatever happens, you always make it be about you."

"That's unfair and untrue."

"I finally meet my father, who you spent my whole life conspiring for me *not* to meet, and right away you're taking him over."

"Taking him over?"

"You just don't get it, do you?" Elena exclaimed. "Why should I even bother coming out? You just want him for yourself, and Grandma doesn't want me to see him at all."

Jen reminded herself that this was the nature of twelve-year-old Elena. A short while ago, she'd blamed this kind of irrationality on Max's appearance in their lives. Now she accepted that Elena could behave like a graduate student one moment and a toddler the next, and sometimes a dual-headed version of both, screaming illogical conclusions in stereo.

"Your relationship with your father," Jen said, "is very important to me. I want you to know him. I want you to be close to him."

"Right," said Elena, as though she'd just heard the world's least convincing lie. "Like I buy that."

"You *are* coming out," Jen said. "You've accepted the gift of a ticket from your father, and you're coming. If Grandma comes, too, we'll all make her feel welcome." Robin might be determined to act like a jerk, but Jen would treat her mother with honor and decency.

Even if it killed her.

"Try bossing me from there," Elena snapped.

"I certainly will try."

IN DENVER, Elena threw herself down on her bed. She *had* wanted to go to California. She'd wanted a special time with her dad, meeting her cousins and her aunts and her grandfather. But now her mother had what *she* wanted instead. Attention from Max.

Just like Elena's grandmother. Robin had to be the center of attention, and Elena's mom was just the same. *He's* my *dad,* she thought again, angrily. Why did everyone else in her life feel that they had to come first?

JEN HAD A HARD TIME keeping her mind on her sister's time in front of the camera. Today, her own role was that of narrator, but she could barely focus on that.

She couldn't forget Elena's baffling behavior on the phone that morning. First, Elena was clearly "telling on" Robin, making sure Jen knew that *her* mother planned to interfere in Jen's life. Then, what was this stuff about Max, her taking over Max, or whatever it was Elena had said?

I wouldn't "take over" her father.

And to think that just days before Elena had accused her of trying to prevent Elena from having any kind of relationship with Max. Now, this. But wasn't it really part of the same thing? Wasn't Elena worried about her mother spending time with Max because she believed that Jen would take up time that Max would have otherwise spent with Elena?

Teresa stood before the rooster-shaped

boulder. Her poise was natural. Jen, who lived in front of the camera, hadn't anticipated that Teresa could be as comfortable in front of it as she herself was. *Don't let Mom's coming here change Teresa's experience.* Because Jen sensed that being here had been good for Teresa so far.

"When I hiked out here, returning for the first time since the fire, I saw this boulder. I remembered it. We deployed shelters at this spot, and because of Salma's injuries we stayed here for a bit when we were finally able to leave our shelters. It made an impression."

Teresa's instructions had been to talk about what had happened that day. Jen was to prompt her, to feed questions that would serve as a springboard for further recollections. Back at the fire house, of course, they would edit the footage.

Max sat on a boulder several feet away from Bob's camera and from Teresa and Jen.

"The fire blew up before we deployed the shelters. I think some of us sensed what was going to happen. Maybe if we'd deployed shelters sooner, we would have been safer…"

Jen thought of the photos painstakingly collected of the other survivors from the east flank. With computer animation, Pete would create images to show precisely where each shelter had been deployed. He would also, she knew, cover any discussion of the placement of Salma's shelter.

But it's my job to prompt Teresa to speak this truth, to say where the shelters lay.

Jen waited to see where Teresa's discussion would take her.

Max is going to want me to emphasize that they were building fire line downhill with flames below. And, yes, firefighters now refuse this assignment when it is given.

"When the fire blew up," Teresa said, "we were down here." She led the way down the slope, and Jen noticed, not for the first time, how steep that slope was. Though she now lived at high altitude, Jen could appreciate how steep the slope would have seemed to the Santa Inez Hotshots on the day of the blowup.

They all followed Teresa, and Max fell into step beside Jen. "I know," he said, "that she's going to talk about the position of Salma's shelter. There was nothing about that in the report of the fire investigation."

"The shelter," Jen hissed at him, "blew over before fire investigators could photograph it. The investigation was sloppy and incomplete."

She glanced up in time to see Max swallow, his features unreadable.

She'd already discussed with Pete and Bob what needed to be done. They must request the help of a fire investigator from Missoula, Montana, to attempt a reconstruction, using science, to show what would have happened to a shelter placed as Salma's was on that day. Max had agreed it had to be done.

They worked for three hours on the slope that morning, filming Teresa and listening to her painful recollections. "When we were given the all clear to leave our shelters, I think we were terrified. I was especially. I knew, from the sound of her voice once we were sheltered up, that Salma had deployed her shelter at an angle to mine, instead of parallel. Neither of us were rookies, and I remember calling to her to make sure her feet were downhill, toward the blaze."

"Shit," whispered Max, behind Jen.

She glanced at him and was astonished to find him glaring at her sister. Teresa, fortunately, did not notice.

Jen couldn't believe Max's response. Didn't he want the truth? It seemed to her that she was hearing it.

"We were all scared, I think," Teresa said, "because Salma had been screaming."

Behind Jen, Max crouched down in a comfortable squat, listening and watching, and maybe his expletive had been for the realization that Salma might have contributed to her own suffering and death. Maybe it was sadness and dismay gripping him.

"When you hear about things," Teresa said, her eyes seeking out Jen, "sometimes they are worse than the reality. The scary thing about Salma was that she no longer *was* in pain. She'd been burned that badly. There was that much nerve damage. She knew she was going to die. And there was that feeling…I was glad she wasn't suffering, but I knew that the absence of suffering was bad news."

Teresa, Teresa, why couldn't you have gone on to medical school? How did things get so badly screwed up?

In her sister, for the first time since the fire, Jen saw nothing but potential. Teresa *could* rise beyond her current situation, whatever its apparent limitations. She had *not* been destroyed by the Makal Canyon fire.

THAT NIGHT, after a communal barbecue dinner on the patio of the house, one of those houses that had been paid for with a human life, Max asked Jen, "Want to ride down to the beach? Go for a swim?"

It was only six-thirty, plenty of light. Jen felt both drained and exhilarated. Teresa's work today had been moving and effective, and she'd looked prettier than she had in years. Bob and Max and Pete and Teresa had spent most of the afternoon editing, and the result had satisfied everyone. Well, maybe not Max...

The swimming trip would give her a chance to talk with him alone, or rather to listen if he needed to talk.

"Sure."

The swimsuit she wore beneath her clothes and motorcycle leathers was a purple maillot which flattered her body. She and Max put towels in his pannier. Before they left, Jen went to Teresa's room to see how her sister was doing.

"Another date?" asked Teresa with a small smile.

"Yes. I guess you could call it that. I just wanted to tell you again how great you were today. You're amazing in front of the camera. A natural."

"Not as natural as you," Teresa responded, "but thank you. It was satisfying." As she spoke, she seemed to turn preoccupied.

"What is it?" Jen asked.

Teresa shook her head. "Nothing that matters. If it does, I'm sure Max will bring it up."

Jen thought of Max's moods, swinging one way, then the other, throughout the day. Did he know something about Teresa or about the fire or *something* of some kind? For that was the sense she'd begun to get almost as if he was biting his tongue about something, a little-known fact he was reluctant to share. Speculation about this made Jen uneasy, and she wasn't sure why, except perhaps that her mother and Elena would be coming that weekend and to Jen it was imperative that they find everything relatively peaceful.

"Why don't you tell me," she suggested, "so I'm not surprised."

"You know, *I* am not your daughter. It's demeaning how you treat me, Jen. You think because your life is so together and you're a newscaster that you have a right to treat me as though I'm Elena."

Jen decided to abandon the conversation before Teresa's accusations became more abusive, which they were likely to do. "So, I'm not sure when we'll be back. Want anything from town?"

"No. I'm good. Bob and Pete and I might go for a drive in the fire wagon."

Jen went downstairs and joined Max in the driveway. She took a helmet from him and tucked her hair inside her coat.

Max's face had a preoccupied expression that reminded her of Teresa's.

"What," Jen asked, "is going on?"

But before she could get an answer, a Subaru Forester turned into the driveway.

Richard.

Max nodded to him curtly.

He'll always blame Richard, Jen suspected.

"Off on the motorcycle?" Richard asked. "Just like old times, eh? I'm glad to see my old hotshots again."

Max's smile was barely polite. "We're just leaving to go for a swim."

"Enjoy yourself. Any chance of my getting Pete to show me today's footage?"

"Probably."

Jen pulled on her helmet. Her questions for Max could wait till they were at the beach.

EVENING SWIMS WERE generally considered not the best idea because of the increased possibility of shark attack, but Jen had never seen a live shark in the Santa Barbara Channel, only dead ones washed ashore, and the only person she'd known who'd been attacked by a shark, up near Monterey, had been bitten in broad daylight. So Jen wondered if *Don't swim at night* was a caution based entirely on an old wives' tale.

In any case, it wasn't yet dark as she and Max swam off the Carpinteria beach half a mile from his family's home. At seven, they floated out past the breakers, alternately floating on their backs and fronts, sometimes treading water.

"So what secret are you and Teresa keeping to yourselves?" Jen asked. "Because none of the rest of us seem to be privy to it."

Max came out of a float and treaded water looking at her, his blond hair dark with water, his lashes seeming very long, very black, very close. "You never knew about Teresa and Richard?"

"About Teresa and Richard," could only mean one thing. Max meant, *You never knew Teresa and Richard were...* But what had they been? Jen managed to sputter, "They were lovers?"

A wave rolled toward them, and they lifted over it as one. Max nodded. "That's my understanding."

"When?"

"Not during or after Makal Canyon. It happened the summer before. You weren't a hotshot yet."

"Did everyone know?"

"Salma knew, and I knew because she confided in me. I doubt anyone else knew. Richard's position in the situation was sketchy at best."

"It's not like he was that much older than her," Jen reasoned.

"Oh, be serious. He was her supervisor. Yeah, he was maybe fifteen years older than her, and I suppose he was an attractive guy back then. Certainly someone who would have seemed interesting and romantic to Teresa."

Jen began to remember things she'd forgotten—primarily that she hadn't exactly been her sister's best friend. They'd never gotten along well enough for that. Too much competition and jealousy, always.

"For how long?" she asked.

"I recall that it was a good part of the fire season. Salma didn't like Richard because of it, and I'm afraid she prejudiced me as well."

"Back then—well, when I was a rookie— I thought you revered him. Everyone admired him."

"Actually, you're right. It's only been since then that I've, well, that I haven't liked him."

"Because you blame him for Salma's dying."

He ducked under the water and came up blinking, his shoulders gleaming from water droplets against his golden skin. "Hard to do that," he said, "after listening to Teresa today."

At least he hadn't suggested that her sister had lied for Richard Grass. They'd been involved long ago, and probably they shouldn't have been, but that didn't mean that Teresa would defend Richard now.

"Do you know how that part of their relationship ended?" Jen asked. "Was it, well, cordial?"

"I imagine one or the other of them got their feelings hurt—probably Teresa. There are reasons why it's not a good idea to sleep with the boss."

"Yes, because he will always have more power than you will."

"Exactly."

It annoyed her to think of Richard Grass abusing his position that way. Granted, it was probably one of those things that just happened. But it was also one of those things that someone—he—should have prevented from happening.

"Well, Teresa never told me about it. I'm not sure she'll appreciate your telling me, either."

"She knows that I know?"

"I have no idea. She had something on her mind that she wouldn't discuss with me— something she figured you knew as well."

Max thought it over. "I don't know what that could be, but I doubt it's this. Salma was sworn to secrecy."

"And told you," Jen couldn't stop herself from saying. "Now, you've told me. Did you tell anyone else at the time?"

"Give me a little credit."

They swam along the coast some distance, heading east and prepared for the tide to push them back west. During a rest stop, Jen told him that her mother planned to accompany Elena to California that weekend.

"Does Teresa know?"

"Yes. I told her."

"I'll be glad to get to know your mother better."

"I doubt it. I mean, you might start with that intention, but she can be aggravating. I've spent most of my life trying hard not to be like her."

"What traits bother you, in particular?"

"Well, she prevented me seeing my father—Teresa and me, I should say—whenever she could."

"You trumped her there."

"Thanks," Jen grumbled. It was true. She'd failed to tell Max that Elena even existed, which was a pretty extreme form of keeping Elena from knowing her father. "It was never my intention," she said.

His brown eyes darted away from hers. "No point talking about it."

"I just told you my mother is coming because I want to prepare you for her possible reaction—her possible behavior toward you, her behavior about everything."

They bodysurfed, finally swimming back to their towels in time to watch the sunset.

As she dried off, Jen said, "So, what are your conclusions about the fire?"

"None of us should have been building fire line downhill. The Canyon Wind Estates should never have been built at that location."

Jen waited for him to say more, but soon realized that she was waiting in vain.

She went to the public restrooms to change into dry clothes. Why did she feel so disappointed? Certainly not simply because Max refused to acknowledge Salma's culpability in her own death. How big a deal was that, after all? What effect did it have on her life?

It has to be pointed out in the documentary.

So far, it was being pointed out. But Jen wouldn't put it past Max to go back and cut out Teresa's remarks pertaining to where and in what direction Salma deployed her shelter. Or to try to edit those comments, at any rate.

She found Max waiting at his motorcycle, and it was in that moment that she understood her disappointment. He was handsome. She was attracted to him. He'd seemed to want to know her better, to spend more time with her.

But he hadn't even kissed her since the night before her birthday.

"Want to go up to the tavern for a little while?"

It was the last thing she'd anticipated. The last of the daylight was fading. "Okay."

With Jen behind him on his motorcycle, he drove up into the mountains, back to the tavern they'd visited on the night they'd arrived from Colorado.

This time, there was live music.

Motorcycles filled the dirt and gravel parking lot and lined another parking area across the two-lane highway. Bikers, male and female, stood outside smoking, drinking, talking. The band seemed to be playing a mix of styles and songs from the previous four decades. As Jen and Max walked inside, they were doing a southern-rock-and-roll version of the Clash's "Rock the Casbah."

The music seeped through Jen and she needed to move, needed to dance. Max looked at her, at shoulders already subtly shimmying, and smiled. "Want to dance?"

"Of course."

They went right onto the crowded dance floor. Jen had changed into her leather halter top after swimming, and now she shed her jacket to dance. She set it down a few feet from her, near the low stage. As she began to dance across from Max, she remembered being an innocent college student, loving to dance more than anything.

Now I like to fight.

As if fighting were the be-all and end-all.

She'd rejected dancing, along with other parts of herself; as if she shouldn't have the right to dance, the right to happiness, after Salma's death and after she, Jen, had made love with Max. After she was pregnant with his child and alone, so alone, always a lone parent.

I was so angry.

But *she* was the one who hadn't told him.

When the song ended, she and Max went out to secure both their jackets in the panniers on his bike. At the bar, they both ordered Long Island Iced Tea. The band began to play "Sweet Home Alabama," and gyrating bodies crowded the floor.

"You look happy," Max said, sipping his drink.

"I'm glad to be dancing." She remembered both his distance at the beach and his unwillingness to acknowledge Salma's culpability. But even more keenly she remembered that he had not loved her because he'd been in love with Salma.

Why can't I get over that? Of course, she *was* over it. The offense had occurred between two different people.

During the band's rendition of "Soul Kitchen," a biker tapped Max's shoulder and shouted to him that his partner was "the most beautiful woman in the bar."

Max shouted a reply that Jen couldn't hear, and she asked, "What did you say?"

"'Anywhere.' Not just in the bar. Anywhere."

Later, they sat outside, watching the lighted tips of the cigarettes of bikers standing some distance away.

Jen decided to challenge him. If he intended to continue defending Salma, she wanted to know about it—and not only for personal reasons. His attitude had a direct bearing on the film.

"So what do you think of what Teresa said about Salma?"

"I don't think she had any reason to lie, to make it up or to remember it wrong. And I think the way the shelter was deployed undoubtedly had something to do with her being burned so badly…"

"But?"

"They shouldn't have been there. They shouldn't have had to shelter up."

"What are you hoping to accomplish? You've said you want to see Richard Grass fired, but frankly I don't think you're going to accomplish that."

Instead of answering, he asked, "Ready to head home?"

Chagrined, because of every hopeful feeling she'd had about him that night, Jen told herself, *You're Elena's mom. That's all you are to him.*

For the first time, she began to see things in Max that might actually hurt her daughter. What girl needed the example of a man who was trapped by the past?

CHAPTER TWELVE

"WAIT TILL YOU SEE the choreography for my solo," Elena told her mother as she climbed into the faded Suburban at the Santa Barbara Airport, helping herself to the passenger seat since Max was driving.

"Elena!" exclaimed Jen, a little surprised by her daughter's rudeness. Robin would surely have expected to be offered the front seat.

"Oh, sorry, Grandma." Remembering herself, Elena began to get out, but Robin said, in a tone dripping with insincerity, "Oh, that's all right, sweetie. I know how important it is for you to be with your father."

Jen read a million things into her mother's tone of voice. It was a voice that told her Robin and Elena had debated the importance of fathers. It told her that Robin remembered Jen's opinions on the subject. How ironic, Jen thought. If her mother could only have known. All her old arguments aside, she might almost count it something of a blessing if Max would fade from Elena's life even more suddenly than he had appeared there.

Once, these thoughts would have made her ask, *What's wrong with me?* These were Robin Delazzeri type of thoughts, thoughts Jen had sworn never to have.

Max is Elena's father, and she has a right to see him, whether or not I like him—or he likes me.

And the last was really the point, wasn't it? Didn't she resent the fact that Max didn't seem completely smitten with her?

For the past two days, since their motorcycle ride to the beach, since dancing at Cold Springs Tavern and coming to the painful knowledge that the kisses on the night before her birthday had been enough for Max, Jen had refused another invitation for a motorcycle ride—this time to a downtown crafts fair. Max hadn't asked again.

"In that case, Elena," Max said, "you should offer the seat to your mother."

"I'm fine," snapped Jen. She climbed into the back seat.

"What did *you* do?" Elena mouthed at her father.

Max wondered the same thing. Ever since their trip to the beach and dancing two nights before, Jen had been cold to him. What had he said, what had he done, to provoke this response in her?

It must have to do with Salma. Salma had died, with Max's unborn child. A fetus, a pregnancy. Jen had given birth to Elena and not told him of her pregnancy out of fear. Fear of rejection.

You and I are going to talk, Jen Delazzeri, he silently promised. Today, tomorrow, soon.

THEY HAD a barbecue that evening. Teresa invited Richard Grass, and Jen watched the two of them with interest. Teresa was no longer a beautiful coed. Nonetheless, feelings of friendship had survived between the two of them. Jen sensed they were often talking about the fire, and when they went out to gaze at the canyon, she followed and joined them. "The fire definitely hadn't spotted below when we started working on that fire line," Richard was saying.

"But we couldn't see it, once it did spot," Teresa pointed out.

A critical point. More than one of the ten standard fire orders had been violated. None of them had to say it, the fact was so well-known. Fire orders, once learned, were not forgotten; not for someone who'd spent even a single summer fighting fire. The first letter of each order spelled out the mnemonic device, FIRE ORDERS, which made the series easy to remember.

Fight fire aggressively, but provide for safety first. Way to start with ambiguity, Jen always thought about that. Safe was *not* fighting fire aggressively, except possibly with air tankers.

Initiate all actions based on current and expected fire behavior. The Makal Canyon fire had definitely gone wrong with this one. Because they hadn't known what the fire was doing.

F.I.R....

Recognize current weather conditions and obtain forecasts.

Ensure instructions are given and understood.

Obtain current information on fire status.

Remain in communication with crew

members, your supervisor and adjoining forces.

There had been bad communication in Makal Canyon; the steep terrain that had made fighting the fire so treacherous had also created many dead zones for the radios.

Determine safety zones and escape routes. Well, that had been done. But when the blowout came, neither group had been able to reach its zone in time.

Establish lookouts in potentially hazardous situations. As far as Jen knew this had not been done at all, a fact no one, not even the fire investigators, had so far addressed. She wanted to ask Richard, but he was speaking; agreeing with Teresa that they hadn't known what the fire was doing.

F.I.R.E. O.R.D.E.R.

Retain control at all times. Jen had spent many hours in many fires wondering just what control meant. Often, her musings had taken her back to Robin Delazzeri, the quintessential control freak, Jen had thought at times. She didn't think so tonight. Robin had been frightened, yes, and her fear *had* made her controlling.

Damn it, I raised Elena, and now he's

stepping in as though he has equal authority in her life...

Not fair, Jen. Not true, either.

F.I.R.E. O.R.D.E.R.S.

Stay alert, keep calm, think clearly, act decisively.

Jen understood now that it was her mother's pain over her rejection by Gino Delazzeri that had led her to use her children as a weapon against him. And that was wrong. But was that *all* there was to it. Though he hadn't driven drunk with her and Teresa in the car, she'd definitely seen him tip back more than a few beers.

Well, you don't have that excuse, Jen, for keeping Max from Elena. She had no valid excuse.

"Did you post lookouts on this fire?" Jen asked Richard.

She saw the hint of reaction before his features smoothed and he began to answer. What was it she'd seen? Surprise? Dislike? "Actually, there was some confusion. It wasn't my role to post the lookouts. Normally, it would have been, but George and I reconstructed responsibilities to fit this fire. That was a mistake."

Massive understatement. Jen wanted this answer on camera. "Let's grab Bob," she said, "and do this conversation on camera."

Richard looked at the Corona bottle in his hand. "I don't know. This isn't my first tonight."

It was certainly his first at this barbecue, and Jen was certain, again, that he was lying. *I'm going to nail him,* she thought, with a barracuda instinct she'd never known she possessed. With his previous answers she'd sensed he was indirectly admitting culpability, admitting that mistakes had been made. Now, he was covering up. And she didn't believe the nonsense about "reconstructed responsibilities."

If he had said, *That was another lesson I had to learn from that fire,* would she have felt more sympathetic? Max wouldn't have, she was sure; but Max wasn't here, wasn't part of this conversation. He also wasn't her.

But she didn't care for liars or cover-up stories. They did too much damage, and the wrong people took the fall for what went wrong. George, for instance; the fire's incident commander couldn't defend himself because he was dead. And if Richard criticized George in the film, family members would be justifiably outraged.

She wanted, suddenly, to talk to Max. But she wouldn't. The last she'd seen him, he was inside charming her mother. Elena was old enough that the courts would listen to her if she said, for instance, that she wanted to live with her father. And Elena *might* want something like that. And she would use it as leverage. It was only a matter of time before she began to voice the refrain, *If you don't let me, I'll go live with my father.*

Jen and Teresa had never had that option, not back then. Jen supposed they could have run away or left home at sixteen, but by then their mother had succeeded in discouraging their father from contact with them; they saw him seldom.

To be a mother was to sacrifice. Not only time, but one's heart. To be big enough to say, *He doesn't love me, but he still loves you.* To say, *My relationship with him has nothing to do with your relationship with him.* To say, *Oh, I'm glad you're spending time together.* To say even one kind word about the other parent, after he'd broken your heart.

Her mother, she knew, had never seen those things as her duty.

"You remember the wildland firefighting safety orders," Teresa said to her sister. "Do you remember LACES?"

Aha. Teresa could spot a hypocrite, too. LACES was the acronym for the essential elements of the safety orders. "Lookouts," Jen ticked off. "Awareness. Communication. Escape routes. Safety zones. So if you look at Makal Canyon from that perspective, all the fire orders were violated."

"There were escape routes and there were safety zones. We used the safety zone. You didn't reach yours because Max chose, instead, to light a backfire—to create a black zone in which you could deploy shelters."

"We could never have reached our safety zone," Jen replied, hearing the anger in her voice, as if someone else had spoken. "Max did the math. He *chose* to light that backfire, instead of opting for all of us to die."

"If he didn't think the safety zone was good enough, he should have spoken up."

"Maybe he did."

"To me. I was his supervisor."

Jen found Max's error in not complaining

about the selected safety zone too minor to mention. She doubted he would make that kind of mistake today. He'd been a squad boss in his first position of leadership on the hotshot crew. He'd done his job well and had saved lives in Makal Canyon on the day of the blowup.

Jen said, "I understand your not wanting to be in front of the camera tonight. How about tomorrow?"

"Can't. Work party."

Jen thought she'd like to be a fly on the wall at that event—if it wasn't fictional.

SHE SENSED Max behind her in the kitchen. She'd come in to make a cup of tea, to get away from the sounds of the party and to think about the documentary—its purpose, its stated mission. *To review the events in Makal Canyon on July twenty-third, 1994...*

"I saw you talking with Richard."

"Do you know how accusing you sound?" Jen asked. "Why shouldn't I talk to Richard?"

"You were talking about the fire. Did you find out anything?"

Jen remembered why she hadn't gone for

another motorcycle ride with Max, remembered his private purpose of removing all hint of stain from Salma's name—or so she, Jen, saw it.

She said, "I don't care for your vigilantism."

"Why are you angry with me?"

"I'm not." But she was. Saying that she wasn't was just denying an obvious truth. She was angry without a legitimate reason. *I'm angry because you're not declaring undying love for me,* was pretty close to the truth, and she definitely wasn't going to tell him that.

"It was just a mistake to—" She stopped. How could she possibly phrase this semilie? *I shouldn't have trusted you?* But what trust had he betrayed? *I shouldn't have let you buy me motorcycle leathers?* But it had been a generous gift. And she liked her clothes. *I shouldn't have read so much into it?*

Why not be honest, Jen?

She was an adult, after all.

"Look," she said, "you're an attractive guy. You bought me some really nice clothes, took me riding on your motorcycle, and I know it's because I'm the mother of your child and you want to be friends."

"These are the—"

She wouldn't let him finish. "I'm susceptible. I'm a single mom. The package you present, not the least of it being that you're the father of my child, is appealing."

"So you don't want to talk with me now? And you think buying clothes for a woman is what I do when I want to be 'friends' with her?"

"And," she said, "you're still emotionally involved with Salma."

"If I had died in a fire after you and I were lovers, wouldn't *you* have remained emotionally involved?"

"You were alive and I didn't," she fired back.

The small, tight smile that didn't reach his eyes was oddly triumphant. "I thought you were 'susceptible.' "

"I'm *newly* attracted to you."

"But you admit that it's partly because I'm the father of your child."

The man was maddening.

The kitchen door swung open and Robin walked in. The look she gave Jen was disapproving, the kind of expression in which disapproval is concealed by false *friendliness* toward the source of the conflict. "Max, there you are."

Here we go, Jen thought. Hadn't Robin been a naysayer whenever Jen had found someone new? Maybe this was just her mother's usual attempt to control every situation around her.

Anger surged through Jen, and it was an old rage. Rage over not being allowed to see her father. Rage over being taken to the women's shelter, of all places, and there being forced to participate in Robin's manufactured dramas. What was the worst part was that *sometimes* Jen had believed her mother was afraid. Which meant that sometimes she'd believed her mother's fear had a reason. Yet her adult understanding of the situation was that her father would never have hurt Teresa or Jen.

Had he ever harmed Robin physically? Jen doubted it. She could imagine her father losing his temper, maybe turning over the breakfast table in frustration, but she couldn't imagine him pushing, shoving, manhandling or striking a woman. That didn't mean it was *okay* to overturn the furniture. That was simply the limit of what she could imagine her father doing. And today it would undoubtedly be enough for a restraining order. But her father's temper had been part of her childhood reality. And he'd found her mother infuriating, Jen knew that. He'd wanted to see his daughters, and virtually every time he tried Robin Delazzeri had been willing to lie and to act to prevent him access.

Often, her mother had said things like, *Well, we could all go to the movies.* She used to call up Gino and suggest an outing involving the four of them, refusing to acknowledge that he was dating someone else or simply that he never wanted to spend any time with Robin that wasn't absolutely essential because she made his life hell and he didn't trust her.

Looking at her mother now, Jen thought, *I'm not sure I'll ever forgive you.*

What if Elena never forgave her, Jen, for not letting her see Max in the first decade of her life?

Max murmured to Jen, "We're not done."

Her pulse quickened, and she wished it hadn't; wished it never would around him.

"You're far away, Jen." Her mother said what her mother had always said when her youngest daughter was daydreaming.

"Not so far," Jen answered without thinking.

Max turned away with a knowing grin and grabbed the coffee decanter, which he filled with water. He poured the water into the reservoir of the coffeemaker and turned to the freezer to take out coffee beans. "Coffee, Robin?"

"No, thank you. I never drink it. Like Jen."

"Any reason?" Max asked.

"Coffee stains your teeth and, in my case," Jen said, "does a nasty number on my skin. In television, neither of these is desirable."

"I can see," he said, "how Elena became so conscious of protecting herself for her career. I just asked her again if she'd like a surfing lesson."

"Afraid of injury?" Jen asked. This trait of her daughter's concerned and sometimes embarrassed her. What if life doled out some injury that Elena was simply unable to prevent?

"Elena is sensible," Robin said rather fiercely.

"Yes," Jen agreed less enthusiastically. "She's sensible. But she's overcautious. You know she is. And no one can stand in the way of life and death. Things…happen."

"Not if you're careful."

How could Robin have made it to adulthood believing this? Jen herself didn't believe it, and she'd known less death than her mother had. It was like people who believed that if they prayed they would receive physical protection from God. Did they think people who were burned or murdered didn't pray? Did they think the victims of war didn't pray? In any mature faith, physical protection was neither the point nor the promise.

She herself rarely prayed, yet she'd had a fortunate life so far.

"Mom," Jen said, unwilling to avoid this particular argument. "What if, God forbid, something happens to Elena? Say she's crossing the street and is hit by a drunk driver?"

"She's too careful for that."

Her mother, Jen knew, would not be persuaded, would not admit that such a thing could happen to one of hers while she herself lived and breathed. But, sooner or later,

Elena was going to have to face the problems that came with being too cautious—and the impossibility of completely protecting oneself from peril. Jen sincerely hoped that her daughter could accept this rationally and that she wouldn't someday have it brought home in more painful fashion.

Robin said, "Also, Elena's a very *feminine* sort of girl. Not like Jen."

"I'm not feminine?"

"Muay Thai is not the most feminine of sports."

"I think Jen is the most feminine woman I know," Max said, and Jen wondered if he made a habit of over-the-top assertions.

"You must not know many women," Robin said.

Mother!

"I *came* to see if you'd noticed," Robin told Jen, "that the chip bowls are empty. They need to be refilled or cleaned up."

This was a challenge, one Jen wouldn't touch. Her mother was no Suzy Homemaker. She never ran after chip bowls, full or empty.

"Actually," Jen said, "Max and I are having a work-related conversation that we need to finish." *And I'm secure enough in my femininity that I'm not taking your pathetic bait.*

"It's a priority," Max said.

"He's brewing coffee."

Jen watched his carefully unchanging expression. Cleft chin, earnest eyes, nothing given away. But she knew what he was doing. Thinking. Thinking about Robin Delazzeri, about her attitude toward him, about if and how he should respond.

"And I don't expect you to grind these coffee beans," he said. "But since we keep being interrupted—" he invented shamelessly "—I thought you might want to run upstairs and change so we can go for a spin."

"Not on that motorcycle!"

Of all the perils in Robin Delazzeri's world, few were to be compared with motorcycles, with the possible exception of trampolines.

Jen knew motorcycles were dangerous. She knew her chances of dying on Max's bike were greater than the chance of dying in an automobile accident. But she wasn't suicidal and riding on a motorcycle driven by an experienced biker, which Max was, did not equal suicide.

"Sure, let me go up and change."

"Could you bring down my stuff, too?"

From his room. He'd never invited Jen inside before. He must really want to annoy Robin.

Well, so did Jen. "Of course, sweetie."

Robin stalked out of the kitchen without another word.

"WHEN ARE YOU GOING to take Elena to meet your father?" Jen asked when he'd pulled up outside the coffee shop where she'd waited for him two days before. He'd left the coffeemaker at the fire house set up with fresh grounds, ready to brew in the morning.

They ordered black coffee—Max—and Sleepytime Tea—Jen—and sat outside watching a red sun set beyond the channel.

"Tomorrow," he said. "I hope you'll come, too. Actually, we're invited to lunch at my father's country club."

"Oh, just a little pressure for everyone," Jen said before she could stop herself.

"Just pretend you're at home and treat him like you would your mother."

Jen burst out laughing. "You're not serious."

"I hope he won't make you feel the temptation. But he may." Max changed the subject. "Let's go back to your interesting statement about my emotional involvement with Salma. I'm surprised I need to make clear to you that she's dead, she died thirteen years ago, and I'm no longer in love with her."

Just as long as no one has to make that clear to you, Jen thought.

He touched her wrist, which lay on the table. "Jen, I'm a little wary of you."

"Why? I'm about the most harmless person…"

"That's how you see yourself?" He burst out laughing.

"How do *you* see me?" she asked.

"Fiery. All fire. Hot-spirited, passionate, quick to fight, quick to get over it. You also know who you are. And you can be a bit intimidating. Tonight, I think I saw why."

"Oh, thanks."

"Meaning no disrespect to your mother."

"Meaning that I'm *like* her."

"What I meant is that survival must have required you to learn to stand up for yourself, for what you believe. And I don't want to hurt you as I did the last time."

Her heart sank. As far as she knew, it was 100 percent true that when someone said, *I don't want to hurt you,* it was because they thought they were going to.

"How would you hurt me?" she asked, telling herself she no longer cared and that he would *pay,* pay for jerking her emotions around after she'd said she was afraid of that very thing.

"By being cowardly."

"Cowardly?" This made no sense.

At that moment, an electronic "Waltz of the Flowers" played. Max grabbed his cell phone. "Our daughter's choice," he said.

Our daughter. If he'd said, *your daughter,* what would her feelings be?

Not good. Maybe she was quick-tempered, as he'd said. She knew she could be judgmental.

"Max," he said and listened. "Yeah… Yeah…" He peered around Jen, his eyes suddenly keen. She swung her head and smelled smoke—distant yet too close. "He just wants us to portray him in a positive light. He wants to be the star. Don't go."

A moment's conversation at the other end. A woman's voice. Teresa must have called him. Jen desperately wanted to know where the fire was, what was going on.

"Makal Canyon's our project, but you're right, Teresa. I can't stop you. Would you please put Bob on?" Listening. "I'm sure he does feel the same way. Would you please put him on?" In the next moment, Max said in a low voice to Jen, "There's a fire in Montecito Hills. Lots of big, expensive homes and an urban/wildland interface."

In other words, the fire was either on public lands or could stray there.

"Richard wants us to go film him being IC, a sort of Where We Are Now."

"Bob absolutely should not go there, not after…"

"Bob?" Max spoke into the phone. "Hey, I don't think you want to be over there. If this has to happen, let Pete film it, and not 'cause I think you can't do it. I know you can. But you don't need to pay that price… I hear you, but I'm still saying no. Please don't do this. Yes. Yes. Yes." After a few moments' conversation, he shut his phone. "He's going. I couldn't talk him out of it. And they're going over there now, while there's still daylight."

"I don't want Elena there."

"Don't you think your mother will prevent that?"

"She'll certainly try. But I think she finds your work romantic, Max. She might want to see…"

"At this point," he said, "with our crew heading over there, let's get to that fire. Then you can take Elena home in the van if she's there."

"But I need to be part of this, too. I need to interview…"

His eyes met hers, and she knew he was thinking that most of his arguments to Bob applied to her, as well. So he dialed Elena's cell phone, and their daughter answered. "Hi, Elena. What are you up to?" A pause. "Oh, yeah? What movie?…. Just checking. You don't belong at the fire. I just wanted to make sure you know that." Elena's voice in the background, terse and probably sassy. "Okay, then. Your mom and I will see you later."

Max shut the phone with a troubled expression, a puzzled expression as well, as though he didn't understand his own reaction to what he'd just heard. "She didn't want to go. They're watching *Love, Actually,* on DVD."

"Good," Jen said. "Why do you look that way?"

"She said she didn't want to come," Max said slowly, "because it's dangerous. She could get hurt."

"That's true," Jen pointed out.

"I guess so."

But she knew he was thinking what she was. That Elena's inherent caution came from an unhealthy source—the belief that if she was cautious enough, she'd have a successful career as a ballerina.

And that wasn't necessarily the case.

CHAPTER THIRTEEN

"THESE PEOPLE ARE HERE with my permission," Richard said to a colleague in a clean fire shirt, as Max and Jen, Bob, Teresa and Pete joined him at the incident command post. He made introductions to his BLM colleague.

It was smoky outside, the kind of smoky haze that Jen knew would filter up to Santa Barbara until the fire was out. In the sudden warm Santa Ana winds Jen had felt outside the coffeehouse, it had grown to 250 acres, and already two homes had been lost.

Jen quickly became absorbed in the project. She felt less tension from Max than she had expected. She knew his private feud with Richard had become a two-way street. She'd heard Richard at the barbecue; heard blame he'd tried to place on Max. Also, Richard was now incident commander on a good-sized fire, and Max wanted to move into that kind of job. So he was judging Richard, but Jen suspected he was still learning from him, as well, even if Max might not admit that.

The timing of the phone call couldn't have been worse. Why had Max called himself a coward?

As they waited at a command post, a sobbing woman walked past, keening.

"A pet," Teresa said.

"Oh, God." Jen's heart ached. *I want to get away from this world.* No doubt the woman had also lost her home, but Jen knew she would especially hate to lose her own cat that way.

"People need to realize," Richard was saying for the camera, "that they must assume some responsibility in where they choose to build their homes."

"We're using that," Jen said to Teresa. "That's the point about Makal Canyon that no one wants to publicly make."

"I mean, if it were me, I wouldn't want anyone to lose his life defending my home," Richard said, "and no one does want that."

Jen stepped forward, "But, Richard, I have the impression that it's more common for fire supervisors to take aggressive action when homes are threatened."

"Absolutely. And that's the right thing to do. But in certain fire situations it becomes impossible to defend structures. That's a fact."

Richard was going out on a limb with his honesty, and Jen was certain his supervisors would not appreciate his candor.

As Richard made a motion for Bob to turn off the camera, he said, "That's all the time I can give you right now, but feel free to stick around."

"Thank you," Jen said sincerely. "What you just gave us was very good."

Yet she couldn't help noticing that the fire, Richard's involvement, and this performance had successfully turned attention from his part in the tragedy at Makal Canyon.

ELENA WAS ASLEEP when Jen knocked lightly on her bedroom door, then looked in. Or that was Jen's first impression. Then, her daughter spoke. "Hi, Mom. How was the fire?"

"Ghastly." And Jen could still smell the smoke on her clothes and in her hair and knew she would smell it when she showered.

She sat on the edge of Elena's bed, and her daughter wrinkled her nose. "I know," Jen said. "I wanted to talk to you about something, but it's late."

"Tell me."

"It's just… Elena, I know you want to be a ballerina. You know it's very competitive, don't you?"

"Of course. But I'm pretty good, and I have time to get better. And if you let me go to a performing arts school…"

"Elena, I just mean that sometimes things happen in life that aren't within your control. I hope, probably almost as much as you do, that you're able to achieve what you want in life. But you could…" How did she voice these concerns to a twelve-year-old.

"Don't count my chickens before they hatch. Grandma always tells me that."

"That's not exactly what I meant. I just want you to live, to have fun, not to feel you have to treat yourself like spun glass. Oh, I don't even know if I'm right, Elena. Maybe you're wise not to do anything that might jeopardize your future chances of becoming a dancer. It just seems to me, sometimes, that you're sacrificing too much. This is a cliché but one with truth: *You're only young once.* There are all kinds of chances. Be careful you're not missing other valuable opportunities in order to secure this one thing."

"I hear you, Mom. But I'm pretty sure I'm doing the right thing."

Jen nodded. She would report this conversation to Max. She bent over and kissed Elena's forehead. "Good night, sweetie. I love you."

"'Night, Mom."

OUTSIDE ELENA'S BEDROOM, she ran into Max. Jen gestured him toward her own room, at the far end of the corridor. Standing in the doorway, she told him in whispers about her conversation with Elena. "I guess I don't think it's such a worrisome trait," she said. "That's all. And I'd rather she was too cautious than reckless."

Max nodded, not disagreeing. "Want to come sit in my room and talk? There are some nice chairs in there."

"Sure."

She followed him down the hall to the room which, in daylight, had a good view of Makal Canyon.

There, she told him about her conversation with Richard at the barbecue and Richard's assertions that George was supposed to place lookouts.

"I don't believe that," Max said. "Do you?"

"No, and I have to admit, it made me angry. We did have a lookout on our side. I just remembered. Bill…" She fumbled for the forgotten name.

"Wiler."

"Yes."

"He had a hard time notifying us, though, remember, he talked about it afterward."

"I remember. I think he actually had a bad battery."

"That was it. He was crying then, but we were all okay on our side, and he'd gotten back to us. He told us about the fire spotting below us."

"Yes. He got burned, too. Just second degree, like you did on Silver Jack. By the way, all healed up?" His look was mischievous.

Hers quelled. "Yes. Completely, thank you."

"Just checking. If you wanted me to look at your injury…"

"Actually, I want you to tell me what you meant by 'cowardly.' "

Max sighed. He sat back in the rocker he'd chosen and put his stocking feet on an Arts and Crafts footstool. "I have a fear of attracting what I fear. It started with Salma. I was always afraid she would get hurt firefighting. If you'll recall, she was the slowest hotshot."

"I don't, actually. What I recall is that she was the most beautiful."

"There was at least one other hotshot who wasn't bad-looking at all." He winked and continued. "So, when she died, I figured I'd attracted it by being afraid of it."

"What are you afraid of about me?"

"Revenge. That if you find yourself in a position of power over me you'll hurt me simply because I hurt you long ago."

"That would be a very small way for me to act. Also, I can't imagine hurting a man just to hurt him."

Max looked as if he didn't quite believe her, and Jen wondered why. She rushed to fill the void and regretted each word as she released it. "Anyhow, hurting someone isn't just hurting them. My innocence is gone. I wouldn't do that to someone, take their innocence about love." Her hand flew to her mouth.

He put his feet on the floor and leaned toward her, where she sat in a chair not four feet from his. "I never meant to do that. I was very young, too, Jen. I didn't know what I was doing to you. I would never have knowingly done that, either."

"I don't know what made me even say it. It's not as though it matters."

"I think we've come to this point several times now and that you may as well stop saying that it doesn't matter." He reached for her hand, and she gave it, almost limply.

I'm terrified, she thought. *He's talking about cowardice, but every time he seems to get close I push him away. Why?*

Because she sensed that he was the One? No. She'd never sensed that about anyone. *Oh, yes you did, Jen. Thirteen years ago.*

But this was *not* thirteen years ago, and Max Rickman was not who he'd been then, and she wouldn't be interested in him if he were.

Why can't you loosen up, Jen? Why do you have to wear single-motherhood like some kind of holy armor?

Because she was Robin Delazzeri's daughter.

"I've lost you. You're far away, as your mother said earlier tonight."

"It seems a lifetime ago." She gathered her thoughts. "It's hard for me to loosen up, Max, to laugh, to have fun. I became serious a long time ago. In fact, I've always been serious, but going straight into single motherhood and an ambitious career path made me even more serious. The other night, when we were dancing and you said I looked happy, it was as if I'd found a piece of myself that had been lost. Then, I thought you were still, well, brooding over Salma, and it disappeared again. It's hard to get back. I don't trust easily."

"I need to talk to you about some things," he said, "and I'm worried about how you may react."

Great.

"I need to see Elena regularly, and she needs to see me."

Jen breathed carefully, not tensing.

"It's her right, Jen."

"I didn't say 'No,' did I?"

"I can see how you're reacting."

"You *cannot* see. You have no idea what it's like to grow up in a quote, unquote, broken home."

"It's not what I want for Elena either, Jen. I'm going to ask you something… Before I finish, know that there are many reasons for my asking. It's not just because of our child."

Jen tensed.

"I think," he said, "we should get married."

"I'm not sure we ever should have had lunch!" she exclaimed.

Max laughed, looking both so handsome and so gently loving that Jen's heart stopped. One of its shells broke away, and she shed just a bit of all that held her back, stopped her from loving Max—or any other man.

He gazed at her. "Think about it."

Jen unconsciously scooted her chair back from him several inches.

He looked down to see how far it had moved on the floor and then back at her face. "You see the problem," he said.

"I do *not* always back away."

"You do more often than you know—and in more ways than you know."

"So you want to marry me because of Elena."

"She's only one reason. But don't you think that would be best for her?"

"*No*. She doesn't need that. She gets along fine without—" And Jen froze, hearing herself, knowing herself. She covered her face with her hand. "Oh, God, Max, I'm sorry. I'm acting like my mother. And she was so wrong. We needed our father. We needed to be able to see him every day, if we wanted to. But we were never offered the choice."

"Wouldn't you like Elena to have the choice that wasn't yours?"

"Yes," Jen whispered, looking up into his eyes. "But she's twelve. She'll leave home in six years."

"And she'll come back for vacations. And maybe she'll get married and have children. And even if the worst happens, and you and I both know that the worst is to lose her in one way or another, then you and I will have each other."

"Oh, God."

He got out of his chair and crouched beside hers. He spoke softly. "We can live together in Leadville."

"She dances every day at a very good dance school. How do you think she's going to react to *Leadville?* It's a mining town. It's small. It's rough. You know it is."

Max knew all of this. Expeditions from various outdoor schools, wilderness programs for juvenile delinquents, so many of these launched from Leadville. But there were ski bums who drank too much, people who'd failed at one thing or another and were running away to Colorado's mountains.

"It's where my employment is," he said.

"I know." *But what is there for me?* Yet Jen knew, knew with certainty, that to do what he suggested would not be confining but freeing—for Elena as well as herself. Elena would fight them, fight like an alley cat with appropriate sound effects. "Okay." She half laughed as she spoke.

"Now, that's enthusiasm."

It wasn't a very enthusiastic proposal.

"Jen."

She lifted her eyes to his, and he touched her wrists, her forearms and gazed into her face.

"I think we can build a good life together," he said. "I believe we'll challenge each other, become better by being together. You have things to teach me."

"And you, me," she replied.

He kissed her. She remembered the taste and shape of his mouth, the slow, careful, tasting caress of each moment, the cautious closeness, the firm desire. She remembered want.

"Max."

"Mm."

They spoke no more, just kissed for some time until he said, "Will you stay with me?"

Stay with him. Make love with him. Sleep with him. "Yes." *I'm terrified, Max.* He had asked her for marriage. They were engaged. Yet she wondered if she would always fear rejection from this man because she'd been rejected by him once.

"You did say," he asked, looking at her, as if to clarify, "that you're going to marry me? I didn't read the wrong thing into that 'Okay'?"

Jen laughed, shaking her head. "You read it right." *I'm happy. A man wants to marry me for reasons he hasn't named—except our daughter—and I'm happy anyhow.* As they moved toward the bed, Jen added, "She's not going to respond well. I guarantee it. She'll say I'm trying to 'take you over.'"

"She doesn't have to like it for it to be the best thing for her."

"I know. But when she's unhappy I feel like a bad mother. And I would be the first person to admit that my duty isn't to make her happy. I like to make her happy, and I want her to learn to make herself happy."

"I think she'll learn that."

"Maybe better now." She frowned. "But there are complications. I live with my mother and Teresa. My mother and I own a house in Denver together."

"Are you saying that she needs your help with Teresa—or that Teresa needs help with her?" He seemed less focused on his own words, his own questions, than he was on undressing her.

"I'm just saying that we've all lived together for a long time."

"Leadville's not far away." Max pulled back the covers, and they lay on the bed together, touching, kissing.

Jen continued talking, almost feverishly, as she lifted up his shirt, as he pulled it off. "And Elena can stay with them when she goes to dance camp. But, Max... I don't know how my mother will react, but I doubt it will be good."

"I don't know how my father will react,"

he answered with a smile. "But none of them can seriously argue with the wisdom of it."

"*Anyone* could argue with the wisdom of it."

Max smiled again. "But you and I aren't going to argue now." He gently silenced her, touching her, gazing at her in the lamplight.

I'm afraid. I'm afraid that if I trust, he'll reject me again. Can people know how much pain they cause?

She wanted to make love with her whole being, holding nothing back, but how could she trust this man, even now that he'd asked her to marry him?

His touch made her forget. She could not think. Only feel. She knew she would risk, was risking her heart. But only because her feelings were already involved. And she savored the closeness and tried to read in him if he felt love for her. If what she believed she saw in his eyes was really there.

It was later, when he held her curled against him, that he asked, "How shall we do it? Would you like a big wedding with our families there? Or something quick and small?"

Jen felt herself relax. And trust. "I'm a big

fan of quick and small, but Elena should definitely be there. I think our families should be."

"Our families are all here right now. When are your mother and Elena going back?"

"Tuesday."

He smiled. "Think we can get a license Monday?"

"There's no one to fax me my birth certificate. No, wait. I was born in Monterey… Maybe it can work."

"I think it can," he answered and she knew he was talking about more than the marriage license. He drew her against him again. "I know it can."

THEY WERE TO MEET his father and two sisters, sisters' husbands and children at the Carpinteria Country Club. Jen dressed in flowing pants and matching long top and vest in white and cream. She wore her hair in an updo adorned with a small spray of white desert flowers she'd picked outside. Elena had chosen to wear her hair the same way, saying, "We've got to stick together, Mom," which had surprised Jen.

Jen and Max had talked about how to tell

Elena that they were getting married. She might be upset, but Max wanted to tell his father when he saw him. So they'd decided that Jen would find a time and way to tell Elena before the lunch date.

My timing's horrible, Jen thought as she turned from the mirror in her room, relinquishing it to her daughter. "Elena, Max has asked me to marry him. And I've said yes."

Elena did not move. Just kept adjusting her dress, a flowing white silk that made her look like a Greek maiden of myth. "Without asking me."

"We both feel this will be best for you."

Hearing her mother, Elena recognized two things. One, that this marriage wasn't happening because anyone had thought about what would be best for Elena. Two, that her parents' marrying each other would reduce her control over her own life.

Trying not to sound *too* sarcastic, she asked. "So he's coming to live with Grandma and Teresa and us in Denver?"

"We're going to live with him in Leadville."

Elena spun from the mirror and stared at her mother. Challenging, and knowing this was a challenge she would win. Because she absolutely had to. "I won't go. I'll stay with Grandma."

"We can decide that later. The wedding's going to happen. We're getting married Monday. But a major point of this is that we both believe it's best for you. So you can have both of us."

Elena said, "I think I'd prefer a traditional broken home, to be honest."

Her mother answered, "I will certainly share your input with Max. In fact, you can tell him yourself."

"Like he's going to care. People don't get married for their kids. People don't even *stay* married for their kids."

Her mother next sounded tart. "Max and I plan to marry, in any case, and plan to stay married."

"I can't believe," Elena heard herself say, and decided that she meant, "that you're stupid enough to marry each other."

Her mother didn't seem hurt, just puzzled. "Why do you think we're being stupid?"

"He doesn't know how unnecessary you think he is."

"I do *not* think he's unnecessary."

"You certainly did for almost all of my life. You're not marrying him because he's my father. Neither of you need to pretend that it's for me."

"It's not," Jen agreed. "But in some respect, it's because of you. And because of other things."

"Such as? Are you in love, or just in lust with each other?"

Her mother looked taken aback. *She probably thinks I don't know what lust is,* Elena reflected. *That's how out of touch she is.*

Jen turned away to study her reflection in the mirror. "Let's go down. Why don't you talk to Max about this?"

"Because you're my mother, and I want answers." And she wasn't going to the country club or anywhere else until she got some. Didn't her mother realize how much pressure was on her, meeting Max's whole family which was also her *own* family.

"I'm your mother, and I want to be treated with respect."

"I don't respect you." She'd probably just gone ahead and slept with Max, just because she wanted to. As far as Elena was concerned, her mother had told her nothing but lies since she'd finally decided to tell Max that he had a daughter. The biggest lie was that she wasn't *after* him.

"You may not respect me, but I still expect you to treat me as though you do."

"Fine. Please tell me everything you can about why you're marrying Max." *And try to tell the truth for a change.*

"Because I believe I can live with him. Happily. Till I die. I believed it when I was eighteen, and I believe it now."

Elena considered this and decided that it did sound like the truth. But she asked, "You really loved him?"

"I loved him. Yes."

"And you do now?"

Jen shrugged. "Things are a bit different now, but he's my friend, and that's what a husband should be."

"Please don't tell me you're really doing this because of me. If you like each other, why don't you just live together? When people get divorced…"

"We're *not* going to get divorced."

"Doesn't it bother you," Elena said and couldn't help herself, even though she knew she was being cruel, "that he doesn't love you?"

"To be perfectly honest, I think he does love me. We're doing something practical, not something romantic. People used to marry for reasons other than love all the time. Marriage isn't really about love, it's about survival. It might be better this way. Marriage is about building a life together."

Elena thought this over. "I think you understand marriage better than Grandma, and you've never even been married."

"Thank you," answered her mother. "I'm sure I don't understand it, but I do believe that what holds a marriage together is an absolute decision to hold it together, and Max and I share that."

"How do you know?"

Was that doubt she saw in her mother's eyes? *Yes,* Elena decided.

"Because we know each other, and though we haven't seen each other for years, we still know each other quite well. Time does that. Also, we worked together as hotshots. We were like family to each other then."

Elena wondered if she could somehow stop them from doing this thing which seemed, to her, completely insane. Also, she knew she wouldn't see *more* of both of them because of it; she would see less. They would just get more wrapped up in each other, and she'd be brushed aside. "I won't move to Leadville. There's no one but backward people there, and I bet the school's not very good."

Her mother said, "It's an expeditionary school. Students go outdoors to learn first-hand about the environment."

"Have I ever done one thing that made you think I'd be interested in that?"

"You've told me that you want to go camping with your dad."

Elena breathed out in disgust and caught up her white woven handbag. "I wanted to spend time with him, and wanting to camp with my dad is different from going to an ex-peditionary school where I don't know anyone. If you cared about me, Max would come live in Denver with us."

"I care about you."

"This was supposed to be *my* day," Elena said bitterly, "to meet my grandfather and aunts and uncles and cousins. Now, it's your engagement day."

Her mother looked tired. "It's no one's day. Let's just go meet your dad's family."

Elena pulled the pins from her hair. "I want to wear mine down," she said, making plain the reason why: *I don't want to be anything like you.*

"AND THIS IS ELENA." Max drew his daughter forward to meet his father, then each of his sisters. He had first introduced Jen, her mother and her sister—the last two included because of the announcement to be made—and his family had said politely that they were pleased to meet them. Elena shook hands with his small nephew and two nieces, as Norman Rickman told her that he saw a resemblance between her and his own mother when she was young.

A white-jacketed host led them through an open dining room with big wide windows looking out on the golf course and the ocean beyond.

Jen found herself seated on Norman's right, with Max's sister Marina's husband on her left. Max's sister Misty sat across from Jen. A waiter came and left menus; then the wine waiter came and took a wine order. As he returned, Jen told Max's younger sister, "I remember playing Ping-Pong with you at a barbecue here."

"I remember, too," Misty said with a friendly smile.

"Jen, now tell me about your work," Norman said, offering and pouring wine into her glass.

Jen explained that she used to work for a news station in Denver but had quit and wasn't sure what she planned to do next.

The retired surgeon's mouth bowed down slightly.

Max said, "This is as good a time as any to make an announcement."

Jen's eyes shot uneasily toward Robin's face. Her mother was straight-backed, beautiful and silently disapproving of everything around her except her own daughters and granddaughter, for which she took credit.

"Jen and I are going to be married. Monday," he added.

Anger immediately covered Robin's brief surprise. She shot a look of outrage at Jen. The look said, *You might at least have told me.* Or even, *You might have cleared this with me.*

Norman recovered first. "Congratulations, Max." He stood and raised his glass. "To the bride-to-be. And to my granddaughter Elena."

It was smoothly and graciously done, and Jen smiled her thanks around the table.

Seemingly seconds later, Max's father, seated again, remarked to Jen, "Well, I suppose Max will be moving to Denver. Your family won't be able to make ends meet on a ranger's salary." He sounded satisfied with what he saw as the inarguable rightness of his opinion.

"We plan to live in Leadville," Jen replied, "and I'm sure we'll manage just fine and that I'll find something to do there."

"It's hard to find employment in those little mountain towns, and you're bound to take a significant pay cut."

"I think it's great!" Misty said. "I'd love to live in the mountains, and Leadville's a cool little town. Keith and I and the kids have visited Max there twice."

Grateful, Jen said, "It will be fun when you come again, when we're all there."

It wasn't until two hours later, when Robin, Teresa, Max, Elena and Jen had all arrived back at the firehouse, from where there was no escaping the haze of the Montecito Hills fire, that Robin said, her voice tight and angry, "I cannot *believe* you didn't give me some warning. Just what do you think you're doing?"

"Marrying the father of my child?" Jen answered. She'd had enough, between Dr. Rickman and her own mother. Max's sisters had saved the day, Teresa retaining a shy silence that had annoyed Jen almost as much as her mother's obvious displeasure at the news of her daughter's coming marriage.

"So you want Elena and me just to show up on Monday and be pleased about this thing. Did you blindside your daughter like you blindsided me?"

"I told her about it before the lunch, if that's what you're asking."

"And you're moving out of my house."

Oh, now Robin was calling it *my* house, which it most certainly was not. Jen ignored that. "We're moving to Leadville."

"Elena won't go. You know that, don't you? And if you try and make her, you'll have more problems on your hands than you ever dreamed of." They stood in the hallway outside Jen's room, where Robin had followed her when they reached the house.

Jen heard footsteps on the stairs, and Max came around the corner of the open corridor.

Robin's mouth tightened.

Jen said, "Mother. It's decided."

"You don't even know what he's after," Robin hissed, "but I can assure you, I do."

Max joined them. "Everything okay?"

Robin composed her features. "I'm astonished that either of you think Elena could possibly be happy in Leadville. She won't be able to take dance lessons there. You're only thinking of yourselves."

"There is a dance studio there," Jen said.

"But probably not a good one," Robin responded.

Max listened silently, and Jen saw a movement at the end of the hall. Elena stood in the suddenly open doorway of her room.

"You know," she said in a low but carrying voice, "it would be nice if *anyone* cared what I wanted. You're no better than they are. You just want to keep your matriarchal dynasty together."

Jen was stunned at the sophistication of this remark and tried to think if she'd ever said anything like that in front of Elena. *Not when I knew she was listening.* But surely Elena had heard Teresa and her do enough talking about growing up with Robin's anti-father tyranny. But still— Jen supposed she could have heard Teresa say that.

"Nobody," Elena said, shoving arms into the sleeves of her windbreaker, which she pulled on over a crop top and white jeans, "has bothered to ask what I want. *You,*" she added, looking pointedly at her grandmother, "will be happy if they get divorced and spend the next six years fighting over me. Then you can give Mom lots of tips on running away to shelters and pretending she's a battered wife."

Elena, apologize to your grandmother. Jen couldn't say it. Wasn't it *she* who should apologize, for talking about the past where her daughter could possibly hear? *I have no idea what to do.*

Before she could say anything—or decide *what* to say—Elena announced, "I'm going for a walk," and strode to the staircase.

It happened then.

In an instant.

Jen saw the toe of her daughter's aerobics

shoe catch on the tile stairs and her calf and ankle extend and twist, as Elena sank with a silent whitening, grasping for the wrought-iron rail and falling.

CHAPTER FOURTEEN

THEY SUMMONED Max's father, who came at once, examined Elena's foot—and a wrist he suspected was broken—and helped her to his car to take her to the emergency room. Jen and Max climbed in the back seat, and Robin, without asking if she was welcome, pushed Jen over and said, "I'm coming, too. I care about her more than both of you put together."

"Would you stop fighting?" Elena exclaimed, tears on her face. "My life is ruined. Why do you have to fight now?"

"Your life is *not* ruined," Jen said. "Get that out of your head right now. We're all sorry you're hurt, and we're going to the hospital, and we'll make certain you get excellent care." But she knew that a tendon injury could be difficult—could possibly be impossible—to repair.

It was Norman Rickman who didn't contribute an opinion. Did he know of Elena's dreams of becoming a professional dancer?

She'll never forgive us, Jen thought in despair. *She'll never forgive any of us.*

Max leaned forward in his seat. "Holding up?" he asked Elena.

And she didn't yell at him. He and his father were the ones she seemed *not* to blame. Of the three who'd been in the upper corridor, only Max was excluded from her animosity and resentment.

Was it growing up in an all-female household that had made Elena so angry now? Or simply that familiarity had bred contempt?

At the hospital, Max got a wheelchair for Elena and wheeled her into the emergency room.

They were at the hospital for four hours, learning that Elena's wrist was broken and her ankle sprained and waiting while she received treatment from Dr. Rickman's old partner.

"I can't do my solo, now," Elena whispered to Jen when no one else was near her bed.

"I know." Jen squeezed her hand beneath the uninjured wrist.

"Can I stay here with you?" Elena said in a low frightened voice. "Instead of going back to Denver with Grandma?"

"Of course," Jen exclaimed. "I would love that, though I'm so, so sorry, sweetie. So sorry this happened."

"Are you sorry you're going to marry my dad?"

Jen shook her head. "Though we'll wait till you're able to stand up. It's very important you stay off your ankle so that it heals well."

"I know. I feel stupid."

"Why?"

"For thinking I could keep something like this from happening. I wanted to believe Grandma, but nothing is that predictable, is it?"

"Elena, all the physicians have said this sprain should heal just fine. Your wrist will heal well, too, especially if you do your physical therapy as you're recovering."

"I'm lucky my grandfather's an orthopedist, aren't I?"

"Yes," Jen agreed, "you are."

"I'm sorry," Elena said, inexplicably.

"For what?"

"For being so rude and bratty."

"I think your anger's pretty understandable."

"If I really hate Leadville, will you let me go live with Grandma?"

"That's up to her, too," Jen pointed out.

"Oh, she'll want me."

Jen was sure her daughter was right.

"Probably," Jen said. "But we'll want you to give Leadville a good try, first. If you feel too anxious about downhill skiing or snowboarding, why don't you try cross-country?"

"Maybe I'll try snowboarding," she said unexpectedly. "I've always been kind of a misfit because I don't board or ski."

"Elena," her mother said, "you never have to be anyone different from who you are—for me or anyone else."

Elena nodded unhappily, no doubt thinking about her solo.

MAX COULDN'T UNDERSTAND his mix of feelings. Part of him knew only happiness and excitement: He was marrying Jen Delazzeri, and she and Elena were coming to live with him, and it felt right, more definitely right than any other life events he could recall.

The film, too, was coming together successfully, and he didn't like to try to narrow down the source of his dissatisfaction with the project. Whenever he did, he knew himself to be at least partly wrong. For thirteen years, he had blamed Richard Grass for Salma's death. The unstated mission of the film—Max's mission—was to make sure that everyone who saw the film knew who was to blame for Salma's death.

But how much was Richard Grass to blame?

Not as much as Salma herself.

Max dismissed this thought. If the hotshot crew hadn't been where it was, Salma wouldn't have died. Period. If Salma had set up her fire shelter correctly, with her feet to the flames, she *might* have survived.

It was the second week in August, and Max knew they'd be ready for a first screening of the documentary by the end of the month. But the question of Salma's death nagged him more and more, and he found himself running away from the answer.

Max himself had urged Salma Garcia to become a Santa Inez Hotshot. He'd spent two summers fighting wildfire. In his final class as an undergraduate, an upper-level environmental chemistry class, he'd seen a beautiful woman with thick black hair. Salma. In their early days of dating, he'd told her about the excitement and satisfaction involved in fighting wildfires.

On the night before the rescheduled wedding, Max accepted a beer with Pete and Bob, then went upstairs and knocked on Jen's door. Though they hadn't spent a night apart since he'd asked her to marry him, she still kept her own room in the firehouse and sometimes retreated there when she wanted to spend some time alone. "Want to go for a ride?" he asked when she answered.

The wedding was to be a fairly casual affair on the beach in front of Max's family's home, with a minister who was a friend of his father's presiding. Robin's departure after the announcement of Max and Jen's engagement, and after Elena's injury and refusal to return with her to Colorado, had been a stormy scene. But she'd agreed, rather grudgingly, to attend the wedding and had flown back to California for it.

Now, Jen gave Max her grin and said, "On the eve of our wedding?"

"Of course."

They rode on his motorcycle to a stretch of beach a mile from where they would be married the next day.

As they sat on the sand together in the dark, watching the glistening, changing shape of foam on each breaker, Max said, "I persuaded Salma to become a hotshot. She was terrified of fire, and I told her she'd feel better if she faced her fear."

"I remember that," Jen said, though she hadn't remembered until he mentioned it. "It helped. I remember her talking about how it helped. You know, various people talked about that a bit when she died, that she'd been afraid of fire and then killed by fire."

Max's eyes showed sorrow. "Teresa told me she'll never forget Salma's screams. She says it was an inhuman sound. But later she wasn't complaining any more. Then they realized what bad shape she was in, as we all did when we showed up."

"Teresa has burn scars herself."

"I know. Does she seem different to you since she's been out here?"

"She seems much better," Jen admitted. "She's thinking about going back to school and studying sociology. Or something. She's done that before. It's possible that my mother encourages her—unconsciously, I'm sure—to be dependent on her, on my mom. She likes to control things. She calls it 'keeping her little nest together.' This is hard for her, our marrying. I don't think she ever really wanted any of us to leave home. It would have been the same with Elena."

"Do you get what I was saying?" Max asked.

"You think it's your fault, somehow, that Salma died?" Jen had wondered for some time if something like this might lie behind his determination to punish Richard Grass. The Montecito Hills fire was long since under control, and Richard had acquitted himself brilliantly, by all reports. But he claimed to be too busy to be filmed again. He knew that Jen wanted to ask him why no lookouts were posted. She would have been more aggravated by his stalling were it not for Elena's injury and her own upcoming marriage to Max.

"Basically. If she'd never become a hotshot, she'd be alive now."

That was true. "She liked being a hotshot,

Max. She said it gave her more self-confidence than anything she'd ever done."

"Really? How do you know that?"

"She told me when I signed on." Jen studied his profile in the starlight.

He turned to her, touched the side of her face, and pulled her down in the sand beside him. "I'm glad I'm marrying you," he said.

And she thought—or imagined—that what he meant was he was glad to be marrying *her*.

Not someone else.

"IT'S VERY EASY to get married," Robin said that evening, as she, Jen and Teresa were closeted in Jen's room. Elena was downstairs playing Ping-Pong with Max. She smoothed the dress Jen had bought for the wedding. Robin had not been part of that shopping excursion—she'd been in Denver at the time— so Elena and Teresa had comprised the rest of the fashion committee. The result was a flowing white gown, sleeveless, with lots of filmy fabric, and a delicate wreath of white flowers for a headdress. Elena insisted that the whole effect made her mother look like a Greek goddess. "It's a lot more effort,"

Robin concluded, "to get divorced. So you better be sure. And his parental rights will be stronger if you've been married."

Jen sank down on the edge of her bed. She gazed at her mother, whose face remained surprisingly unlined for someone her age, her eyes dark, intense and burning with a curious charisma that had always attracted friends and acquaintances. "Mom, I really need to say this: Please stop fighting me about Max. Please stop trying to interfere with his relationship with Elena—and with me, for that matter."

"I'm not trying to interfere. I'm just urging you to be cautious. You don't know how helpless you can feel when you're trying to protect your child from influences you could never have guessed were there when you were first getting to know someone."

Teresa, whose blond hair had grown during her stay in California, and who'd lost ten pounds and been hiking every day, spoke. "Just what influences were you trying to protect Jen and me from? What was so bad about Dad?"

"You don't understand anything about that situation," Robin said tensely. "He was with a nineteen-year-old girl when you were children. She even got pregnant, but she miscarried or had an abortion or something. You can't expect…"

Jen had never known any of that, but she burst out, "Well, you just have to be bigger. I'm sorry. That must have been horrible, Mom, but it didn't have anything to do with us. We wanted to see our dad, and you used us to try to punish him."

"You sound about thirteen years old," Robin said tightly, "but Elena is more mature than you."

"You tried to control everything," Jen went on, like a fountain that would not stop spraying water. "It wasn't about what he'd done to you…or done, period, because he wasn't necessarily doing it to *you*. And, Mom, he never hit you. We felt like idiots going to battered women's shelters, and here you're putting on this act…"

Robin had gone white. She began to shake, and Jen knew what was about to happen.

"You don't know *anything*," Robin said.

It occurred to Jen that perhaps she didn't. Perhaps, alone with her mother, her father had been another person. Yes, she had heard her mother lie, relate events that she, Jen, had witnessed, in a completely false way. Once, she had known her mother to do something to herself in her bedroom, hit herself with something, and come out with a black eye. But that didn't mean Gino had never hit her.

"You're a good mom," Jen said gently, assuming again her role of caretaker. Of Chief Liar. "You took care of us mostly alone, though Dad did pay child support."

"Only if I *made* him. Only if I told him he couldn't see you otherwise."

"Which is illegal."

"I had a moral right to protect my children from him and his values."

Robin was dead wrong. *And I understand that she's wrong,* Jen thought. *My understanding of what she did wrong will prevent me from becoming like her.* Not for the first time in her life, she prayed that she was right about this. Should she quit arguing with Robin? She would never win. She could try her whole life and never win.

But Teresa said, "So unless he was who you wanted him to be, he couldn't see us."

"It wasn't who I wanted him to be." Robin

seemed to be starting to hyperventilate. "It was who I know he could have been."

And the Chief Liar took charge, so that there wouldn't be a Robin Meltdown. "You're right, Mom. You always wanted the best. We love you."

Her childhood was long over. Robin would never change. But Elena, by God, was going to know and spend time with her father.

JEN LAY AWAKE. How could she be so certain that marrying Max was what she wanted to do, what she was somehow *meant* to do?

Because it was what she'd wanted long ago?

No. Not that simple. If Max had not changed, had not grown into exactly the man he'd become, she couldn't have agreed to marry him. It wasn't who he'd been but who he was and who he promised to be that spoke to her.

And yet…

Max had spoken tonight of some sort of reckoning he'd managed. Coming to terms with having been the one who'd encouraged Salma to join the hotshots in the first place.

Now, Jen remembered when Max received the news that Salma was dead and afterward. Things said.

Things done.

Things felt.

Her own opportunistic certainty—doubt free—that there was nothing whatsoever wrong with her being in bed with Max.

Part of her still cringed as she remembered the young girl she'd been. *Salma's dead, he's free.*

And she, Jen, had always liked him, always looked up to him, always envied Salma. Like the kid sister who suddenly has a chance with her older sister's sexy, mature boyfriend, Jen had seized her opportunity to be closer to Max.

What had gone through his mind?

Probably just horror that Salma was dead.

But that wasn't what he'd said at the time.

So many things she'd spent years blotting out, deliberately forgetting, she now remembered. Chance remarks. Fragments. *That smile,* he'd said of hers as though his heart was breaking at the beauty of one facial expression—hers. Hers, not Salma's.

Also, when the two of them had kissed,

there'd been a sweetness. He had not acted as a practiced older seducer but as someone entranced by her.

Back then, she'd have been thrilled had he wanted to marry her. But it couldn't have happened back then. Some things could only happen with the passage of time. If she'd been asked about the critical factor back then, thirteen years earlier, she'd have said it would have been for him to get over Salma. Now, she knew that wasn't what had to happen. She'd needed to grow up and not need him in the way she had, in the days after the fire, to make her complete.

So she'd raised a daughter alone, had a career, stood beside Teresa through her struggles. Now she was mature enough for marriage. Now she was independent.

Now she was ready.

A knock on her door.

Jen got up, pulled on some sweatpants with the Leadville smoke jumper T-shirt Max had given her, and opened her door. It was Max.

"Am I stealing your beauty sleep?" he asked.

"Of course, but I'll survive. I'm glad you're here."

He came in, shutting the door behind him as Jen switched on her bedside light.

"I'm getting back in bed," she said.

She'd talked him into spending the night apart from her so that he wouldn't see her in the morning, thus—by traditional superstition—causing unluckiness. But now he came and lay down on the bed beside her.

"If I leave before midnight," he said, "can I stay?"

She almost laughed. But now that he was here… "I'm glad you're here, because there's a question you've never really answered."

"Mm? What?"

"You've said you're not marrying me only because of Elena. What are your other reasons?"

He rolled on his side to face her. "Has it escaped your notice that I'm very attracted to you?"

She grinned, the feel of the smile surprising even her. "Still, these days most men don't see marriage as a necessary step to resolving that."

He gazed into her eyes, his own creasing in the corners, following his smile. "No," he agreed. "I guess we don't." He paused. "Do I love you? Yes. Is my decision about love? Not really. Marriage, to last, should be built on other expectations. Or hopes. I see you and I being able to share things, to grow together. We'll always have common interests. I think it can work. Does that make sense? We can truly be partners, not just in raising Elena."

"Yes." So he loved her. Now he had said it. That must be enough.

She related the scene with Robin in this bedroom only an hour before.

"Teresa told me. She said she always forgets that your mother is never going to change."

"I always forget it, too."

What she wondered now, however, was how much time would have to pass before she changed, before she believed that he was marrying her for reasons that truly had to do with who they were together as a couple, not simply as Elena's parents. How many days or months or years would have to elapse before she didn't see the two of them being together now mainly—if not solely—because of their child.

CHAPTER FIFTEEN

EARLY THE FOLLOWING MORNING, Max walked into the computer room to find Pete uneasily scanning the first page of a fax which was still spitting subsequent sheets onto the paper receiving tray.

"What is it?"

"Nothing you need to look at this morning."

Taking this as an indirect sign that the fax was important—critical, even—to the film, Max moved closer and read over Pete's shoulder.

The previous week, they had sent an independent fire investigator in Missoula, Montana, photos from the Makal Canyon fire, particularly of the fire shelters. Of course, Salma's shelter had been moved from the place where it had lain during the fire, as had many of the others. The precedent the South Canyon fire had set weeks before, of leaving shelters—and the dead—where they lay had not yet made itself widely felt. And in any case the priority would have been helping Salma and others who were injured.

But the fire investigator revealed that at fire research laboratories in Missoula, he and other fire specialists had examined enhanced photographs of the site where shelters had been deployed and had found they could see depressions in the ground at approximately the spot where Teresa Delazzeri had indicated that Salma Garcia had deployed her shelter. Deploying a shelter in that direction, he continued, would greatly increase the risk of fire entering under the shelter and burning the firefighter inside.

The pages of the fax gave scientific data and evidence to support the findings.

The fax dealt only with the issue of the deployment of Salma's shelter. Other previous reports had addressed the decision to build the fire line downhill, which the investigators had strongly criticized.

Max handed the first page of the fax back to Pete. "I guess it's not that surprising. But we have other pieces to put together. Jen wants to get Richard back in front of the camera."

"Ain't gonna happen. He knows what she's after, and he's not going to say on film who was in charge of assigning lookouts."

"Not the IC," Max said. "There's no way it could have happened as he told Jen at the barbecue."

"You know more about the fire world than I do, but I tend to agree, just because of the incident commander's degree of responsibility. Will Richard be at the wedding?" Pete asked.

"He wasn't invited." Jen hadn't suggested it, and Max didn't want him there. When all was said and done, the responsibility for Salma's death could be spread around, but Richard Grass had done a lousy job for his hotshots at the Makal Canyon fire. *We need him on film one more time.* But Max knew of no way to accomplish that. They needed his compliance, his agreement.

Pete said, "What about the other guy? The guy who didn't die, but who was involved in a lot of the decision-making? Dick somebody? Isn't he supposed to be back soon?"

"Dick Henry. He is back. He just hasn't had time to talk yet, he says, and I tend to believe him."

"Are you flying him out here?"

"He hasn't agreed to come. But I think he may. The problem is, he and Richard are still in contact."

"Do you know him?" Pete asked.

Max shook his head. "I barely remember him. He was overhead, he wasn't local. We were, which usually doesn't happen on a fire like this, and we didn't know him."

"So all this can wait till tomorrow," Pete finally said. He was to be Max's best man. "Let's get ready for this wedding of yours."

THEY GATHERED on the beach at 11:00 a.m. Jen and Max had chosen vows from a selection offered by the minister. At the time, as certain as she was that she wanted to marry Max, Jen had wondered, *How can it matter what vows we choose?* Max was not in love with her, and no words spoken on the beach in the morning would make him love her.

But now, on the beach, everything *was* different. Max stood across from her in white linen trousers with a black silk shirt in a subdued Hawaiian print. She'd felt silly for caring about this moment, for feeling excitement. She'd told herself that to care so much about this wedding was to be attached to the past, to keep alive a nineteen-year-old girl and her immature love for the Max Rickman of then.

But she'd been wrong. This was not the long-ago Max. Their twelve-year-old daughter, Max's and Jen's, stood near Teresa, Jen's witness and maid of honor, and the reality of Elena, of the years Jen had spent raising her, of the chance that Max would actually have done his part, that she, Jen had done something she had no moral imperative to do... All these things overwhelmed her now, embodied as they were in the present-day Max, her lover and the man she loved. Both of them were different people—the same souls, yet grown and changed.

Jen listened to the ocean as much as to the minister's voice as the ceremony began.

Robin looked tense and disapproving.

Jen and Max had each selected one reading which was secret from the other, a wedding gift to be revealed during the ceremony. Jen had chosen something from a book of the minister's, *Weddings of the Heart*. The excerpt was by William Meredith:

In Chota Nagput and Bengal
the betrothed are married with
threads to mango trees, they marry the
trees
as well as one another, and
the two trees marry each other....

Jen liked the reference to trees and to marrying trees, as Max was not just a firefighter but also a ranger.

Teresa read Jen's selection, and Jen watched Max's satisfied smile. Then, to Jen's surprise, Robin stepped forward in the semicircle of guests, a piece of paper in hand.

"Max asked me to read this poem today. Oddly enough, it has long been a favorite of mine. 'The Country of Marriage,' by Wendell Berry." Robin's eyes grew moist as she began to read, and through the cynical thought that Robin couldn't bear the dramatic spotlight focused on anyone but herself, Jen saw her mother as a hopeful bride, wanting her marriage to Gino Delazzeri to put down roots, to branch upward, to scatter its seeds, to become every rich and beautiful thing a marriage could be. And she felt the stirrings of forgiveness for the wife and mother who had continued to want these things and been denied them.

Had Max foreseen all this in asking Robin to read this passage? It was at moments such as this that Jen foresaw an especially fulfilling future between Max and her. He didn't want strife, but a deeper understanding of all around him.

And through the reading he'd chosen, Jen understood her mother perhaps better than she ever had in her life.

The vows were simple, traditional, straightforward, but their simplicity brought Jen a sense of the peace and the sacred. "I, Jen, take you, Max…"

DICK HENRY FLEW OUT the following week, at Max's expense. Max was the only one of the group who had ever even met him before.

Jen cleared her mind of Max's continued feelings of vengeance toward Richard Grass and of her own worries about Elena and how she would really do in Leadville.

She asked Dick Henry, "Did you and Richard Grass and George Riley post fire lookouts?"

"That would have been the superintendent's responsibility, particularly for the crew he was working with. The squad boss on the other crew should have posted their lookouts."

"But it didn't get done."

"That was a mistake."

THEY FINISHED editing on August twenty-eighth and celebrated with a screening in the living room of the firehouse, which they would be vacating in two days.

"It doesn't matter," Max said, "that he isn't fired. He won't go any further up the ladder with this film out there. Maybe he'll be forced into early retirement."

Jen didn't like what she heard in his voice, the vengeful streak. For a time, she'd been sure Max was ready to move past his rage about Salma's death. She knew he didn't idealize Salma's memory—or, she supposed, she hoped that he didn't. It was easy to see how he could look at what might have been and see how it lacked the problems of what was.

What frightened her was that somehow *married* lovemaking with Max brought them into even deeper intimacy and, with that, greater love and greater trust. He had destroyed her trust once before, and it had only been partially rebuilt. That was the nature of the fine fabric of trust. And Jen no longer saw his desertion of her thirteen years before as something he'd done to her, but rather as something that had happened. His fiancée had just died, he hadn't been prepared, his world was in turmoil. She had been a casualty of the situation. He hadn't been able to help his feelings, and the part of her that had known that at the time must have been what kept burning a single ember of her feelings for him.

The night of the screening, when they went to their room, they talked briefly, as it seemed they did every night, of the logistics of Elena's and her move to Leadville. Then, Max said, "Thanks for making the film happen, Jen. I wanted that on film. I wanted the fault shown."

The film had noted several factors that had led to the disaster that July day when the Makal Canyon fire had blown up. Builders and firefighters together had discussed the development of Canyon Wind Estates and the inevitability of the subdivision being threatened by fire.

The lack of lookouts had been noted—and the fact that the firefighters hadn't known what their fire was doing. Salma's wrong deployment of her fire shelter and her inability to keep it over herself had been addressed.

Jen had watched Max's face during the screening. He didn't love Salma anymore. He loved her memory, of course, as one loves any friend who has died.

But that night, when they were in bed and he took her in his arms, she stiffened some without meaning to.

"What's wrong?" he asked.

"Are you going to move on from what has happened?" she asked. "Are you always going to carry anger over this fire?"

"Why?"

That wasn't the answer she'd been looking for.

"Because you'll never be able to move on, as long as you do. I thought the film would get it out of your system. But you feel the same as you did when we sat down together in the Mexican restaurant in Ridgway and you first asked me to work on the film with you. It hasn't changed you at all."

Max heard her, heard the wisdom in her words about moving on. He could tell her the fire was by no means the driving force in his life. But wasn't that untrue? Wasn't his whole career somehow bound up by the catastrophe?

But what *could* make him move on if the film had not? If he was ready to leave the scene of the fire, figuratively as well as literally, the change would have happened naturally.

"Jen, you're wise," he said. "Be patient with me. Think of it as a habit I'm trying to break."

I didn't agree to marry that habit.

But she had. She'd agreed to the whole package of Max Rickman, and the Makal Canyon fire was part of it.

CHAPTER SIXTEEN

By the end of the first week of September, they'd settled in Leadville and Elena had started school there. She was off crutches and healed of her injuries, but was only dancing in a limited way until she regained more strength. Jen found a part-time job with the recreation district teaching kickboxing, a less disciplined sport than Thai boxing, and was doing some freelance television work as well.

Although Max remained attentive, both to her and Elena, Jen could not rid herself of the feeling of waiting for the other shoe to drop.

In the second week of September, it did.

For Jen.

Maybe it would have been a small thing. She happened to see the credits running after a showing of the film at the ranger station where Max was working. A group of hotshots stationed in Leadville for the long fire season not quite at an end had come in to watch it. Jen was at the station to meet Max. They were going to dinner later, and she saw the credits, which she'd never seen before.

Before a listing of any of the people involved in making the film were the words:

This film is dedicated in loving memory to Salma Rose Garcia. No one will ever replace you in our hearts.

Why hadn't she been asked? Hell, why hadn't she even been *told?* Because Max would know how she'd feel about it?

She didn't know what to do. It was a small thing, she was overreacting, it made no sense to want to run to the restroom and weep and vomit. After all, for those who'd loved Salma, the dedication was no doubt true. But Max was not simply one of those who'd loved Salma. His relationship with her had been more.

There was nothing she could do. She wasn't going to run home to mother over this. It was a *small* thing, a nothing.

Max came out of the back room at the station, his coat in hand. He'd left his California motorcycle in California; he had another here, but today he and Jen were using her car. She wordlessly handed him the keys.

As they walked outside, leaving the hotshots behind, he said, "Should we go home and clean up first? You look great, but I could do with a shower." He rubbed the razor stubble on his jaw.

"Whatever you want," she said, making it a point to smile some as she spoke. It felt like a death grimace.

"What's wrong?"

There was no point in avoiding the question. She climbed into the passenger seat. When Max had slid behind the wheel and shut his door, she said, "I didn't know about the dedication to Salma, that's all."

"Teresa and I wrote it."

"I'm sorry. I suppose I have some residual jealousy or insecurity."

Max eyed her carefully. "I've noticed."

"I'll try to do better," she said without enthusiasm.

"Jen. Don't let it get in the way of us."

"There's no real 'us,' Max. You married me for Elena and you'd have preferred to have Salma, but she died."

"That's what you believe?"

"There's nothing to make me think other-wise."

"So you want me to spend my life trying to convince you of things which can't possibly be proven, but have to be taken on faith?"

"Of course not. Can we just forget this? Let's not let it ruin our evening."

"I think it has the potential to ruin more than one evening. I'd prefer to deal with it, now," Max said, with no pleasure or leniency in his voice.

"There's no way of dealing with it, Max. We both have issues. We just have to accept that this is the way it is."

"But, Jen, you're running on misconceptions."

She waited, hopeful.

"First, I love you and have chosen to spend my life with you."

Just words.

"I am not pining after Salma. Yes, I'm still angry about the fire, but the anger's hard to get rid of. I'm working on it."

She continued to wait, to wait for him to say what he'd married her for, besides Elena, but the words did not come. Nothing came.

She said, "Look, we're building a partnership. We'll have to work with what we have over time."

"Fine," Max said tersely. "Just out of curiosity, why did you marry me?"

She might as well say it, even if she could only say it bitterly. "Because I fell in love with you when I was nineteen, and when I was thirty-two it happened again."

His hand reached out, rubbed the back of her neck. "Maybe something like that happened to both of us, Jen. Did you ever consider that?"

What she considered was that if it was true he wouldn't have said "maybe" or have turned it into a question.

WITH SOME OF HER SAVINGS, Jen invested in a high-quality video camera of her own. She'd decided she wanted to learn to be behind the camera as well as in front of it. Using what she'd learned working on the documentary of the Makal Canyon fire, she began using her free time to produce an hour-long documentary on midwives in Colorado's Rocky Mountains. She contacted Channel 4 with the finished product, and it aired before her first wedding anniversary. They asked her if she'd be willing to do more shows on mountain women, and Jen agreed to three more.

Max was gone most of the time now, smoke jumping. He'd planned for the previous season to be his last, and now Jen wondered if that had been all talk, if he planned to keep jumping out of airplanes until the mandatory retirement age of fifty.

He and Jen had bought her a motorcycle of her own, and she used this in her traveling for filmmaking. Her newest project was on women working in traditionally male occupations in the mountains. She had followed, filmed, and interviewed a snowplow driver—praying for early snow so that she could get footage of this woman at work—a tow-truck driver, a miner and a carpenter. She'd heard rumors of a woman logger living near Buena Vista. On the day before the anniversary she wouldn't share with Max, who was on a fire in Alaska, she headed south to try and find out more about the logger. Elena had been spending most of the summer with her grandmother and aunt, dancing in Denver, but was still certain that she wanted to return to high school in Leadville, where she was becoming a good snowboarder.

Jen was passing a line of cars when an SUV pulled out of the line to pass, as well.

As she flew through the air, she thought, *This is how it happens, then...death.*

HE WAS FILTHY, unwashed for five days, fighting what had become known as the Blizzard Creek fire. Soot, ash and grime caked the creases around his eyes. Sometimes when he stopped sawyering for a few hours' sleep, he took out Jen's and Elena's pictures and thought of his life in Leadville, which now seemed more dream than reality.

Finally, on his wedding anniversary, his group of jumpers was released from the fire and he began the long packout with the others. They were two miles from the road when they were intercepted by the incident commander.

"Max," he said, stopping, guiding him away from the others.

Max knew that it wasn't about the fire.

"Elena," he said. "What's happened?"

"Who's Elena?"

Thank God. Thank God. "My daughter."

"Max…"

Something bad. Something very bad. Not Elena, please not Elena.

"It's your wife. She was hit on her motorcycle."

Dead. Jen's dead. His heart seemed to split, his world to flatten to nothing. He saw her vibrant smile in his mind's eye.

"She's in a coma."

THEN SHE WOULD NOT DIE, and he would not have to remember the moment when he was sure she was dead. But as he sat on one plane after another, heading back to Denver International Airport, all he saw over and over was the blazing flash of her smile, and it was as if she'd been taken from him.

Teresa met his plane. "Elena's at the hospital," she said, as he swept the heavy pack he'd carried over his shoulder.

"Just tell me about Jen." *Tell me about Jen. Tell me she'll be the same as she was. Tell me she'll be at all.*

"She's in a coma, and for now there's some brain damage, but the neurologists aren't saying how bad. They don't know, since she hasn't woken up, which isn't good."

Jen! A scream inside him at losing her, at losing her smile.

He'd never even seen her spar in a genuine Muay Thai match.

"She broke her neck and many bones, and they feel good about the surgery they've done there, except that they can't wake her up."

Max found he couldn't talk. Teresa seemed to be watching his face, calculating what was there.

Absently, he said, "What are you doing?"

"Working part-time for social services in Lodo and going to school."

She seemed far better. Maybe Jen's not being in the home had been good for her, forcing her to take on more responsibility for herself and even for Robin.

But Max couldn't think about it long, couldn't think.

Just Jen's smile.

SHE WAS NOT SMILING, but he knew her hair.

Otherwise she lay as still as if she were dead. A machine rasped for her, and Max clutched at his daughter as Elena, like someone three times her age, began to say what each machine was for.

He needed to be alone, alone with Jen, and a nurse seemed to realize it.

"Let's have one at a time, sweetie," she said.

And his eyes grew wet.

He did not cry.

He grabbed the chair, took Jen's hand.

No response.

Maybe he'd thought that if he came, if he was here, she would wake up.

Had it been like this for Salma? But she'd been conscious. Things shut down one at a time, with Salma.

"Jen." He bent over a rail just to have his head, for a moment, touch her arm. It was awkward. "Baby."

A breath. But something breathed for her, didn't it, hadn't Elena said that? Elena who had been crying, who was afraid her mother would die.

JEN MOVED through a dream in which she was dancing, dancing, and then she saw Max's eyes, crying beside her face, or not crying but wet, yes, crying.

"Jen."

His eyes on hers.

Pain. Everything strange. Not dancing.

Where was she?

Just Max.

Max saying, "God, I love you. God, I love you. Don't ever leave me, Jen. Don't ever leave."

And someone saying other things. "Confusion... Needs to be..."

Strangers' faces. "Jen, you're in the hospital. You were in a motorcycle accident."

Max. Max. She tried to say it and couldn't.

But someone was holding her hand.

She felt the calluses.

She knew.

She knew that something that had troubled her, a very big thing, was gone. And as she felt another touch, like a butterfly's, and heard, "Mom?" she knew that Max and Elena were both there.

She heard Max say, "I don't want to leave."

"You don't have to leave," someone said. "Go ahead and talk to her."

He did. Again. He talked about how much he loved her.

EPILOGUE

ELENA DELAZZERI-RICKMAN, age fourteen, had believed for years—and still usually believed—that she was destined to dance with one of the world's finest companies. She had not believed, two years earlier, that her parents' marrying each other was a brilliant idea or that it would last. But now the idea that it *wouldn't* last seemed impossible to her. Never, until about six months earlier, however, had it occurred to her that she might ever have a sibling.

And now she did. John Norman Delazzeri-Rickman—Jack—was nine pounds one ounce, and had tons of dark hair, but otherwise looked almost exactly like Max.

He'd been born at the little hospital in Leadville, and Elena had seen him being born. She loved holding him and watching her mom nurse him, but when her dad picked him up and held him what she felt was a little different.

She lived, she sometimes thought, in a world of miracles. That she *hadn't* destroyed her chances of being a dancer when she'd had that bad sprain in California, but even more that her mother had walked away from surgery after that motorcycle accident, that she had been okay. Lots of physical therapy and some time coming back from her head injury, but it was amazing to Elena that they were all together and fine. And her dad never went away in the summer now, as he had that first summer.

So she had no reason to feel anything but grateful for every aspect of her life.

Except when she saw her dad holding her little brother.

Then, he looked up and saw her looking at him, and Elena could tell he read her mind and wished he wouldn't. Her thoughts made her feel small, and she'd prefer no one would guess them.

He was sitting on her mom's bed in the birthing suite—which was basically one room in the hospital and nothing special. He said to Jen, "Do you want to take him?"

"Sure."

Then, *they* looked at each other, and Elena thought they might be mind-reading, as well, because that was how well they seemed to understand each other. As though they'd always been together.

"Elena."

It was her mother who spoke, as she held Jack, put him to her breast.

"What?"

Her mother looked up. "I'm sorry, Elena. I'm sorry I made the decision I did. Because your dad would have been there."

"Mostly," her father said, "he's very glad he's here, now." He met Elena's eyes. "With you."

Elena went over to the bed and sat between them and touched Jack's tiny hand and felt her father hug her shoulders and her mother clasp her arm. "Thank you both," she said. "I love you. And I love Jack. God, he's so cute."

She basked in the happiness of her family's love, in this moment of their togetherness in perfect joy.

* * * *

Look out for the next book in this mini-series:
Dad for Life *by Helen Brenna*
is out in July 2008. Don't miss it!